Derelict America

Jeremy Void

"… waiting obsessively … such as sporting large spikes on your leather biker jacket and a torn T-shirt that you tossed in the path of a lawnmower while working landscaping one day … with the gear crammed in the backseat and between Jack and myself, who were seated in the middle seat … so intriguingly disgusting that I can't look away … Amanda sprayed with the steaming water from the blast: stinging her skin … *not a word spoken as they delved downstairs, four black briefcases dangling from four left hands … ignoring him outa spite for his stupid suggestion, because Billy's great & Gregory's being a total buzz-kill, & then things start moving & the party's only picking up … roaring fiercely, as if a strip of fabric is torn in half, each stitch pulled apart, the sound magnified as if my ass is an amplifier, my butt cheeks fluttering … leading into a manic guitar riff and a heavy drumbeat that sounds like a fast clock [***ticktockticktock***] plugged into murderous subwoofers … as if the plane were completely still and connected to a rod that riotously rocked the cabin … cruising in the left lane on Rt. 9, passing cars on my right, listening to Anti-Nowhere League, staring out the open window and enjoying the wind on my face … each and every one of them dressed from head to toe in tie-dye … and with me still holding the button the spray would slam the spider into the wall and I would continuously blast the spider with the lethal liquid … during which the two of them got very very drunk, the following hours feeling like a blur … an umbrella in one hand, protecting her from the pouring rain, and a bundle of roses in the other … 'I know, but what's the point' … but the gesture still deeply penetrates my heart, leaving a permanent hole, in which a safety pin still lingers …"*

Derelict America

A Collection of Short Stories

Jeremy Void

This book is a work of fiction. Names, characters, places, and incidents either are products of the author's imagination or used fictitiously. Any resemblance to actual events or locales or persons, living or dead, is entirely coincidental.

Derelict America

ISBN Number:
978-1-60571-180-5

SHIRES PRESS
4869 Main Street
P.O. Box 2200
Manchester Center, VT 05255
www.northshire.com/print-on-demand

Building Community, One Book at a Time
This book was printed at the Northshire Bookstore, a family-owned, independent bookstore in Manchester Ctr., Vermont, since 1976. We are committed to excellence in bookselling. The Northshire Bookstore's mission is to serve as a resource for information, ideas, and entertainment while honoring the needs of customers, staff, and community.

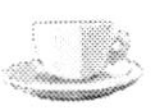

Printed in the United States of America
using an Espresso Book Machine
from On Demand Books

To Kristen

To Lethal Erection

Table of Contents

Go to:

www.chaoswriting.com

Read at your own risk....

Acknowledgements

[A special thanks....]

A SPECIAL THANKS TO ALL those who made this book possible—to God for blessing me with this brilliant ability to absorb and then manipulate both words and grammar; to Kristen for her general love and support; to Tomás and Robert for helping me by way of therapy (and for giving me honest feedback, both good and bad, about my stories); to Steve for putting up with me and not kicking me out of the program (and for giving me honest feedback, both good and bad, about my stories); to Kim for helping me get in touch with Debbie, the publisher, and for giving me general support where needed; to Debbie, of course, for being willing to both publish and sell my book at the Northshire Bookstore; to my parents for not giving up on me when they could have so many times; to my dad specifically, for sharing with me the dream that inspired "R.I.P.: William Taylor, 1997"; to Chuck, my partner in crime, for accompanying me on some of the misadventures that inspired some of these stories; to Janis and Sharon for facilitating a group for writers and allowing me to attend and for the general feedback given to me to better my stories; to the rest of my Creative Writing group; to the cop who arrested me and had me sent to Vermont, where I was able to find peace of mind and pursue my dream to be a writer; to Lethal Erection, for I wouldn't have been able to do this without having played in a Punk band for however many years; to ELF, my newer Punk band; to Thurston for the vote of confidence he has in me; to the Boston Punk scene—"This one goes out to the Punks: we RULE the fucking world"—to those from my past, such as Dr. Wechter, Dan Falvey, and Clinton, for attempting to get through to me and failing miserably as I just wasn't ready to listen yet; to William Noble, my creative writing teacher, for introducing me to writing fiction; to all my other teachers for teaching me skills I wouldn't have known otherwise; to anybody else who supported me along the way; and, last but not least, to all those who doubted me and thought of me as only a fuckup who would amount to nothing. Again, thanks for everything. And just because (if) I did not mention you specifically does not in any way, shape, or form mean you were not important in the making of this book, because I could not have done this alone.

Introduction

[A brief history....]

MY WHOLE LIFE I HAD never liked rules, but circumstances had forced me to conform. It was either conformity or one cot and a box—as in prison. Now, without Lethal Erection, my old mode of self-expression, I was living in a vacuum, basically. In a rut. Rutland, VT, to be exact. So I started to journal, and this act managed to pacify me somewhat. I would write about what I wanted to do to certain people who pissed me off, and in doing so, I dumped my anger into a notebook that no one but me would see. It was brilliant. How I started journaling is a funny story. If I were to have an idol I would pick Richard Hell. I have a book by him called *Hot and Cold*, which is a collection of poetry, short stories, essays, journal entries, pictures, et cetera. I was reading his journal, probably after ingesting a large sum of Ritalin, and in it I read, "If you bring yourself to write for long enough you'll eventually say something interesting." What made this quote special, along with all the other quotes in there that I could identify with, was that I could *identify* with it, for what he wrote encompassed all that I had felt, as if he and I are one and the same.

I always wanted to be a legend, always wanted to have said or done something memorable. I thought the only way to do this was by being absolutely bad; a subterranean vandal, I guess you could say. But that quote by Richard Hell offered me another way to gain notoriety—by writing. So from then on I wanted to write a book.

I didn't yet know I wanted to write fiction, though. I knew nothing of the sort. The only book I'd ever read and finished, I had read a year earlier, and it, too, was by Richard Hell. It is called *Go Now*. When I took English Comp. at the Community College of Vermont (CCV), I had to read John Steinbeck's *Travels with Charley in Search of America*. I didn't read it, though. I refused to. Rather than do what was required of me in class, I winged it when it came time to take the test. Surprisingly, I got a B in that class.

A couple of months later I decided to look up a book I had read only the first few chapters in and give it another try. The book is Christopher Moore's *You Suck*, the sequel to his *Bloodsucking Fiends*. Following *You Suck*, I read *Bloodsucking Fiends*, then *Bite Me*, the third installment in that trilogy. I learned to love reading, and after reading every book by Christopher Moore, I searched for more books by other authors. (You see, all the books I was given to read in school sucked, and so I thought all books sucked.) I went on a binge that consisted of me reading about two novels a week for the next two years. Reading is awesome, especially when the author pulls you into the story, because unlike in movies, in books you get to feel what the characters feel. I don't read as much as two novels a week anymore because I have more stuff going on, but I still read a lot.

So, in the next semester I took Creative Writing, which was not how I'd expected, and English Comp. 2. The English Comp. 2 teacher said if I'd keep it up she could definitely envision me having my own book in only a few more years. Still, though, I had no clue as to what I wanted to write my book about. I had an idea, which was a series of rants about this-and-that called *Everyone is a Cunt*.

It was Creative Writing that brought my goal more into focus. I took that class because I like to write, but I expected it to be more of a free-write kind of thing. One year in high school my English teacher would write three topics up on the board and for the first fifteen minutes of class we had to write about one of those topics—I received a *Creative Writing* award at the end of that year. I expected Creative Writing at CCV would be the same: we would be given a topic to write about and we would write about it however we wanted.

But no, I was wrong. I learned that on the first day, when the teacher asked everyone in the class why they wanted to write *fiction*. I didn't have an answer because I didn't know yet that that's what I wanted to do. My answer was something like, *I write everyday*—meaning, journaling—*and I really like to write*. A lot of my classmates were confused by that response, later asking me what I write about when I write every day. I knew by that point what the class was all about, and so again I didn't have an answer.

I wrote my first short story in that class, getting a B- on the first draft and an A on the final. I was quite proud of that result. I showed that story to everyone.

What I liked most about Creative Writing, the first thing the teacher had taught us was there are no rules in writing fiction. *Ding, ding, ding, we have a winner.* Finally I had found anarchy. I had searched all my life for this. I wasn't an anarchist, though, but far from it. I claimed to be a nothingist, or as some call it, a nihilist. I wanted chaos, as the song by my band ELF goes, "Kill and let kill—we want chaos. Kill and let kill—how can you blame us? Kill and let kill—total mayhem. Kill and let kill—it's all that makes sense."

There are, however, guidelines to writing fiction: where am I? who am I? and what's happening? And those I can live with.

So my writing signifies something very special to me, something very personal, something from the heart. I don't write to entertain others, although it's a bonus when I do. Writing to me is a lifejacket. It has saved my life on many occasions. To not write is to die. So in reading these stories my goal is that I will share some of myself with you, that we will become lovers and fuck until the very end. Some of what you read may be painful, some of it may be scornful, and some of it may be humorous. But overall, I can guarantee, this journey into my mind will be well worth it.

ENJOY!

Sarah's Bedroom Window

A short story....

"... waiting obsessively ..."

YOU ARE SECRETLY HIDING IN the bushes peering through binoculars focused on Sarah's bedroom window. You are waiting desperately for Sarah. Waiting obsessively. A car pulls up to the house and you refocus the binoculars on the car. A blood-red convertible with yellow lightning bolts painted horizontally on the side. A man and woman exit the car. Zoom in. Focus. You can only see the back of the couple's heads, but you recognize Sarah's glistening brown hair, which hangs freely. The guy has short-cropped hair and is wearing an ugly blue letterman jacket. The couple is walking to the door holding hands, you notice spitefully. And they enter. You are so angry, you could just scream. Zoom out. The door gets smaller and so does the house. You aim your binoculars at Sarah's window on the second floor. An old wrinkly woman is taking off her bra. Gross! Wrong window. A little to your left. An empty room is in your view. Pink walls. A pink bed. A pink dresser. A pink desk. Pink, pink, pink. Pink! You crave pink. You wait. You lick your wet lips. Drooling. Oh, beautiful Sarah. She enters her room as you watch. The guy follows her in holding her hand. What the fuck? Who is this guy? With the binoculars focused, you watch as the guy throws Sarah on the bed. He mounts her. It looks like he is sucking out her soul, sucking her dry, his lips pressed to hers, her soft succulent lips welcoming him as he dry-humps her, his body like a snake, her feet in the air, legs forming a V. Your face turns red. Steam rises. Your blood boils. With his hands like claws he tears open her blouse, the buttons ripping apart, two mountains jutting out in perfection, a pink bra ... pink! As he removes his repulsive letterman jacket you watch angrily. He lifts his shirt over his head. A six-pack. Pecks. Biceps. Muscles bulging in every direction. He slides her skirt down her legs as she lays waiting. Pink panties. He is back to gorging on her spit, dry-humping. From behind he unhooks her bra. Tears it off. You want to kill him. Cut off his head. He has no right to fuck your girlfriend. Only you have that right. His lips wrap around her left nipple. Suck. Her pink nipples. No. She appears to be moaning. Shifting her body. After a second or two he switches to her right nipple. No. Back to her mouth. You picture his tongue caressing hers. You curse your imagination. He tears her panties off. She is shaved like a baby's bottom, as you expected her to be. He kisses her belly button, then moves south, where he licks and licks and licks and sucks her clitoris. She squirms. He licks. She twists. He licks. She turns. He licks. You squirm. He licks. He stands up as she sits up on the edge of her bed. Unlatches his belt. Pulls. His belt slips through his belt loops and with the momentum, flies through the air and lands on the floor. She tugs his pants, pulling them down. She does the same with his black boxer shorts. His erect penis sticks out. It is bigger than you expected. Much bigger. Ten inches and thick. She wraps her lips around his erection. Bobs her head up and down. Sucks. You cannot take it. You put your binoculars away, store them in their case. You storm through the bushes and charge to the front door. Surprisingly the door is unlocked and you let yourself in. You are intensely angry. You storm upstairs and nobody stops you. Nobody is to be found. You pull a box cutter from your pocket as you kick down Sarah's door. You are overtaken by pink as she slides her head off his shaft and gazes at you. You, standing in the doorway. You, gripping a box cutter. You walk into the room casually.

"Who the fuck are you?" asks the asshole you are about to murder.

Freedom in America

A personal essay….

"… such as sporting large spikes on your leather biker jacket and a torn T-shirt that you tossed in the path of a lawnmower while working landscaping one day …"

SAY YOU DRESS IN COUNTERCULTURE clothing, such as sporting large spikes on your leather biker jacket and a torn T-shirt that you tossed in the path of a lawnmower while working landscaping one day because you were curious about what the outcome might be, like what kind of design would develop in the damage, and through the wreckage people can see your messy tattoos that were done with a safety pin in someone's crummy basement. Your hair, too, is messy, with clumps of soap that look like cum stuck to the strands, and your eyes are blood-red. On closer inspection one can see the red veins zigzagging like streaks of lightning from the outer rim of your eyeball to your blue pupils that are so bright they actually accentuate the redness. But that's not why you see red. No, it's not. You see red because you and two friends were forced against a wall by the police for no other reason than the way you were dressed—and because a kid played basketball with your head one night outside of Store 24; he dribbled your skull on the cold concrete, making murderous threats. He would have killed you if it weren't for the cab driver who saw it all happen. Of course, those are not the only reasons you see red. Those are only two examples from your life. I mean, you can't forget the time your cool older brother invited you to hang out with his friends because your own friends ... *what friends?* ... and in one of his friend's front yard you took a terrible beating from the bastards while the kid's dad just watched it go on, thinking, you assume, that boys will be boys and that it's not a big deal, they're only rough housing, playing around. To you it sure didn't feel like a game. *YOU WERE ONLY A LITTLE KID!!!* Or do you remember the time you were on the swings while your sister swung on the swing next door, and she dropped her McDonald's toy? Do you remember the two kids who took it off the ground, and when you asked for it back, the taller of the two launched his fist into your gut and you fell to the ground crying? You were in so much pain. That was before the rebellion developed deep in your heart. The anger and frustration you feel first showed itself when you were in ninth grade attempting to fit in, and you wore all the right clothing and walked and talked just like them, but your sad attempts at acceptance only gave you a blackened eye and a swollen lip. So you gave up, and your infamous streak of disorder started from there, and the beatings from bullies and cops continued, only today you are true to yourself and you at least fight back, having developed in your heart a sense of dignity.

Today I can rightfully make the claim that I am free. Or I am almost free. We all have that possibility, though in accepting it comes a responsibility to others. I was talking to someone just the other day, and we both came to the conclusion that as long as there are others of us, other humans, we will never be free, as everything one does will undoubtedly affect at least one other living person. And is that freedom? There are two kinds of freedom: a physical freedom, which we don't have, and a mental (or creative) freedom, which has unlimited possibilities. I am going to focus on the latter form of freedom, and briefly mention that physically, we will never be free because everything we do will impose on a more inferior type, those with fewer cells bouncing around their brains—no offence, if you belong there—as Friedrich Nietzsche wrote: "What serves the higher type of men as nourishment or delectation must almost be poison to a very different and inferior type" (Nietzsche 42).

That is also the premise for Plato's "Allegory of the Cave," in which Plato tells a tale of a guy bound in chains who breaks loose and leaves the cave for a higher calling. At first when he finds freedom, a detrimental fear festers in his mind. But after his eyes adjust to the light they no longer burn and he can accept what he has found, which is so wonderful that he feels compelled to share it with the rest of the men contained in that cave, although they are not ready to hear what he has to say, not ready to accept the truth because it's safer inside the dark and dreary hole they have gotten to know so well (Plato 528-535).

The constant beatings I received and perceived as pointless had given me a higher education than most. But I am faced with the undeniable fact that my peers disliked me, thought I was weird, and labeled me a queer. It was a torturous era, one that I can't relive, though I would rather die than go back in time. The persistent torment pushed me to a point of no return, and when the bad fight began, I felt as if I was free, however false that feeling may have been. Chuck Palahniuk wrote:

> *"The Danish philosopher Søren Kierkegaard defines dread as the knowledge of what you must do to prove you are free, even if it will destroy you. His example is Adam in the Garden of Eden, happy and content until God shows him the Tree of Knowledge and says, 'Don't eat this.' Now Adam is no longer free. There is one rule he can break, he* must *break, to prove his freedom, even if it destroys him. Kierkegaard says the moment we are forbidden to do something, we will do it. It is inevitable"* (Palahniuk, Monkey Think, Monkey Do 213).

I felt like I would get beat up no matter what I did, therefore dressing counterculture couldn't and wouldn't cause my life to take a different route. My peers forbade me to be free, and so standing up for myself while tearing down the lives of others in a lucidly destructive fashion, as Kierkegaard claimed, was inevitable. But that, I later learned, doesn't equal freedom, for fighting the system the way I wanted only made me a black sheep. And if it was inevitable for me to spit in the eye of beauty, if it was predestined, how could I possibly be free? That in effect would rid me of choices. I was everything they were not—yet still under their jurisdiction.

But there was one thing I had that couldn't be contained. And that one thing was called Lethal Erection, my band in Boston. We lived faster and we played louder. This is how it happened:

> The show went off without a hitch; a cyclone of bodies, with flailing arms and legs, danced in a circle to the loud out-of-sync rhythm that rattled the floor. My eyes peered down at them from my post onstage. Behind me Johnny Pain pounded the drums. To my left Kristen smashed the bass. And to my right Chuck hit the guitar, his hand strumming the strings so fast that it looked like a blur even to me as I craned my neck from him to the crowd. When the song gave me the go-ahead to start singing, I moved the mike in front of my mouth, and spit splattered the steel receiver as I senselessly abused the back of my throat, words escaping me in a rapid-fire frenzy of shrill shrieks, my body in a spasmodic disoriented seizure-like trance, falling down and then flailing on the floor. As I thrashed my arms and legs, shaking like a vibrator, members of the crowd clawed at my clothing in an effort to lift me back up. But I was relentless, moving too fast to be contained.

That right there is freedom. That sense of accomplishment from playing a show, from getting up in front of all those people and serving your heart on a platter—that, nothing else can beat. I, St. Chaos, was responsible for writing all the rotten lyrics as De-Chuck-Tive dabbled with the manic melodies (before that it was Jeremy Acid) and Johnny Pain added demonic drum beats to the crass noise pollution that Kristen Epileptic blanketed with the slapping of her bass.

Sadly, though, it all ended when I came to Rutland, Vermont. I kept telling De-Chuck-Tive and Cardinal Erection, the current drummer, to keep it up, for I would be back someday. That was three years ago and as you can see, I haven't gone back. Not yet, at least. However, I still consider myself to have creative freedom. I have successfully found a way to channel the disharmony that hammers inside the confines of my skull. I have found a way out, for I am a writer—a writer of fiction, that is.

By telling tales of terror I have crafted "fabulous," as Yvonne Daley called one of them at the Green Mountain Writer's Conference, stories of murder and mayhem and rape and dope and ghosts that will grab you by your collar and not let go until the very end, and even then your mind will be racking over what had happened, as my stories will steal you from a life of peace and harmony and nail you to a cross, where tiny creatures will crawl all over your flesh, feeding on your brain. That is freedom. That is the best kind of freedom, as nothing can beat creativity. In a nonfictional short story by Chuck Palahniuk, Marylyn Manson says, "The only fear I have left is the fear of not being able to create" (Palahniuk, Reading Yourself 158). Nothing—

nothing at all—can take away a creative mind. Not in America, at least.

After the infamous Holocaust, however, Germany passed a law that limited the mind. It was a law preventing fascism, which is fascism in itself. The idea was that nobody could make a move towards the likes of Nazis—National-Socialists—and things like the Swastika and Punk rock were prohibited. I wouldn't have been able to walk the streets in those days without getting into trouble, which would give me even more of a reason to do so, as that is the point of Punk rock, to say *Fuck you* to all those who oppose your way of thinking—as in everyone.

In America, though, nobody can stop me from wearing a jacket that states CUNT RAWK and POGO YOU FUCKERS on the back and HATE down the sleeve, nor has anyone ever successfully stopped me from wearing a swastika or A PRODUCT OF A BUSTED CONDOM or FUCK ROCK & ROLL or—you get the idea—scrawled in Sharpie on a white T-shirt. People have, however, gotten in my face and forced their ideas down my throat in an attempt to intimidate and have actually assaulted me in an effort to enforce an unwritten dress code that our culture has created as another way to try and control.

But that's all they can do: try.

So if you think we have no freedom, think again.

Works Cited

Nietzsche, Friedrich. *Beyond Good and Evil*. New York: Random House, Inc., 1966.

Palahniuk, Chuck. "Monkey Think, Monkey Do." Palahniuk, Chuck. *Stranger Than Fiction*. New York: Anchor Books, 2004. 4.

Palahniuk, Chuck. "Reading Yourself." Palahniuk, Chuck. *Stranger Than Fiction*. New York: Anchor Books, 2004. 13.

Plato. "Allegory of the Cave." CCV. *The Dimensions Reader*. Vermont: CCV, 2012. 8.

Concentration Summer Camp

A short story....

"... with the gear crammed in the backseat and between Jack and myself, who were seated in the middle seat ..."

MY BAND WAS TO PLAY tomorrow night at Terry's Tavern, and Jack and I were scoping out the scene. We had taken the train to Central Square and followed the directions to Wendy's, where we currently stood right outside the front door, and where we saw through the windows people sitting at booths eating their food. A long line started at the register and in big strides, zigzagged to the dining room, where the line ended. The front door opened, and two black boys and a black girl walked out in single file. They rounded where we stood and I could hear their chatter as they walked behind us. Their chatter faded, and we were still there staring into the store.

"We must have followed the directions wrong," I suggested.

"It says we're playing here," Jack said.

"No way."

"Well, not here," he corrected. "Not in Wendy's. Of course not. But in this exact spot."

I was stupefied.

"Let me see," I said, and he passed me the paper. "You're reading this all wrong," I told him.

"What do you mean?"

"Look." I showed him the slip and said, "According to this, we're supposed to somehow walk *through* Wendy's."

"But," he said, "we can't just walk *through* there."

The door opened and two big white boys came stomping out and they turned not toward us but the other way and for some reason my eyes stayed on them as they walked along Mass Ave.

"I know," I said. "We have to go around."

"Around? What do you mean, 'Around'?"

"I mean around."

"Let me see that!" he demanded, and swiped the slip from me. "Ooooh!" as if it all suddenly made sense. "Follow me," and I did.

We started left, walked all the way to the next crossroad, and stood on the corner as he tried to make sense of the directions.

"I think," he suggested, warily. "I think we should turn right."

"Are you sure?"

"No, I'm not," still focused on the paper in his hand. "Yea," he blurted. "I'm sure."

"Okay, then," I said with a shrug, and the two of us turned right and followed the street to another crossroad that ran parallel to Mass Ave. "Another right?" as that would make the most sense.

He nodded, and we went, passing a parking garage on our left, three stories packed full of cars and vans and various other vehicle, all connected by a ramp that ran from the top to the bottom in a spiral similar to toilet water. That comparison caught me off guard, and I giggled.

"What?" Jack said, and our eyes met. "What's so funny?"

"What?" around a mouthful of laughter. "Nothing's funny," I lied.

"Okay," he said, and we were beyond the parking garage, now passing the back of first Burger King and then Wendy's, both on our right side, and on our left side were beat-up buildings, run down from years of disuse. No sign of Terry's Tavern anywhere.

"Man, are you sure this place even exists?"

"Yea, I'm sure of it," Jack exclaimed.

"I hope so, considering you booked the show."

"I didn't book it," he clearly lied.

"Then who did?" I asked, knowing damn well that he had lied.

"Pauly."

"Pauly Shits?"

"Yea, from Concentration Summer Camp," Jack said.

We were sitting on the curb directly behind—at least that was what we assumed—Wendy's, and across the street was a door towering over some stone steps, really eerie-looking.

"You don't suppose ...?" I stopped myself, then said, "Never mind."

"What?" with curiosity flaming in his eyes.

"Never mind."

"No, really. What?"

"Okay, okay," and finally asked, "You don't suppose that's Terry's Tavern?"

"That?" he said, with a pointed finger.

"Yea."

"Couldn't be."

"It's possible though, you gotta admit."

"Yea, I guess," and he stood.

We both crossed the street and on a paper sign in black Sharpie were two words, those which we were looking for: TERRY'S TAVERN. This was it.

"I guess we found it," I said, and Jack said, "I guess so."

THE NEXT NIGHT WE SHOWED up in Mike's car, with our gear crammed in the trunk and the backseat and between Jack and myself, who were seated in the middle seat, and coming from the speakers was Cock Sparrer. The car rumbled and roared as we passed the parking garage, spewing steam from under the hood. Loud sounds like gunshots blended with the music, making it sound so much better, the four of us thinking it was all a part of "Riot Squad."

We were approaching the venue and no one was there, it seemed. But when we pulled up out front there was a little black woman, with her hair pulled back into dreadlocks, sitting on a stool by the door. Mike rolled down his window, letting splashes of smoke escape, and waved the woman over. She got up and obeyed Mike's command. She was really short, maybe five feet.

She stood by the car, and Mike shouted over the noise, "Where can we park?!"

She pointed up the road. "Go straight, then take a left. You can park on the side of the street somewhere," surprisingly loud enough to be heard.

Mike's window slid up and kept anymore smoke that tried to escape in the car. A coughing fit tore at my throat just then, just as we slowly rolled in the indicated direction, then left, and followed the road, passing car after car on both sides as we searched for a spot. I swear we searched for thirty minutes, because back at Terry's Tavern more bands were unloading equipment and disappearing through the door. With us we carried our instruments but not our amps because the hike we had taken from Mike's car was too far, and we didn't have the lung capacity.

So Jack held his cased guitar in his hand and Harry held his cased bass and Mike scratched his back with one of his drumsticks as we approached the same black women from before. I didn't carry anything as we went through the door, because our mike was broken and Concentration Summer Camp had agreed to let us use theirs.

INSIDE TERRY'S TAVERN MY SOON-TO-BE girlfriend, Caitlyn, came up to me and said, "You've got a problem."

I looked at her and her eyes said, *Don't kill the messenger, Dude.*

"What?" I said, turning back to my band, who were all setting up our instruments as we were on first, and I flashed her an all-knowing grin that said, *Everything will be cool.*

"It's Harry," as I walked over to him and he was seated against the wall, his face red with pleasure, his head hanging on by a thread.

I kicked his flaccid right foot.

"He's out cold"—she spoke to my back. "I've been trying to wake him."

I whipped around, and she took a step back, must have seen something evil in my eyes.

Then my frown flipped upside-down, and my lips lifted into a smile before I wrapped my arm around her waist and pulled her close, screaming, "Somebody get her a bass," and somebody did, a bass suddenly in her hand, her fingers wrapped around its neck.

My gaze gripped her tight, then switched to my band, who had finished setting up and were ready to play.

I STOOD ON STAGE, LIMBER from the booze I drank, and from the amps different notes fluctuated, seesawing from key to key as Jack and Caitlyn synchronized their instruments. Standing on stage, with an antsy crowd before me, I thought that now would be a good time for jokes.

"How many Punks does it take to change a light bulb?"

"Shut up!"

"Yea, shut up!"

"Aaaah"—a pause for emphasis—"four: one to screw it in; one to hold the ladder; one to talk about how Punk this is; and one to call everybody a poser and leave," and I laughed alone, dull stares and drooping jaws and silence....

That was when the first cord of the night, of the show—a guitar cord—sank into my skin, as brutal as a vampire bite, powerful, long lasting. Then cord number two, followed by a steady drumbeat, made the earth quake.

The crowd started to sway. It was great.

As the song sped up, the people who had come to see us made a circle and were skipping, it seemed, along the edge, with swinging fists and high-flying boots and skateboarding shoes, people being pushed out and then pushed back in, some falling on the floor and then lifted up just to be thrown back into the cyclone of bodies that had overtaken this place. Up front others were pogoing—hopping with an erect body—and all over, onlookers watched. Something fierce was flashing in their eyes. Hunger, it looked like. Hungry for what, I couldn't imagine. My cue was coming. I stayed silent, waiting, watching the crowd.

I looked at Caitlyn, who was smashing the bass as fast as she could, and she must have cut her fingers on the strings or something, because blood stained her cuticles.

Then my cue finally came.

I was floating on air, abusing my throat. The lyrics coming so naturally that the song sped by my mind so quick.

I noticed the crowd eyeing Caitlyn, and I started to feel jealous of them. I also noted something glinting in their mouths, something growing.

Something that looked like fangs.

No, impossible.

I eyed Jack and with my head indicated the onlookers, hoping he could see what I had seen. The guitar cut out then, only the bass and drums now. He must have seen it. The bass then followed Jack's lead, and so did the drums.

"What gives?" said Caitlyn, coming over to us. Mike was still seated behind his drums.

My eyes left Jack and rounded the venue, then settled on Caitlyn, who stood on the other side of me, her arms crossed, seemingly angry.

"Why did you stop playing?"—fiercely.

"Look," Jack said, and nodded toward the crowd.

"Shit."

"What do you think's going on?" I asked.

"I have no—"

"Hey!" Mike shouted.

He got up and joined our huddle.

"Look," Jack said, and I noticed that Caitlyn had unfolded her arms, her beautiful brown eyes filled with fear.

"At what?" Mike said.

"Them," Jack pointing with his head again.

"What about them?"

"Don't you see?" I said.

"No, what?"

"Look," Caitlyn said, and something smacked me in the head.

Everybody was yelling obscene threats and throwing bottles. They were ravenous.

We all faced the crowd, like soldiers before a battle, standing there with each other. We were a team. I was frightened.

They started forward, and it was right then when I was sure that those were fangs descending from their gums.

Jack began whipping his guitar in an arc, using it as a weapon to fend against these fiends. So did Caitlyn. Mike and I were backpedalling toward the wall, and something fast flew by my right side and Mike was gone. I looked over my shoulder and there was Mike, pinned to the wall behind his drum set, a fiend on top, licking its own lips. It looked at me, and I looked away.

This was bad, absolutely terrible. Four of them were on top of Caitlyn, ripping her to shreds—and I should have said, *Soon to be dead*. It seemed only Jack and I were left.

Standing side by side, we walked backwards.

I heard a grunt, then a *thump,* and from behind me Mike said, “Hey, guys, I’m still alive.”

I turned his way, and on the floor before him was a dead body, in his hand a bloody drumstick that had been split in half and maybe used as a stake. He joined us to help fight off the approaching vampires when an idea hit me. “Break your guitar on your leg,” looking straight at Jack.

He shook his head.

I nodded *Yes.*

He shook his head again.

Yes, yes, yes, my head gesture said.

And there it was, with a burst of sparks and splinters and a grin of dismay on Jack’s face, the three boys in the band with their backs against the wall and a brood of vicious vampires closing in….

My Eyes Open

A short story....

"... so intriguingly disgusting that I can't look away ..."

"I'M BRADLEY, AN ADDICT AND an asshole," I announce.

"HI, BRADLEY!" eleven addicts chant. I'm sitting in a big bright-lit room. The windows are dark. Scattered around the room are eleven small round tables, each surrounded by four to five metal folding chairs, all in close proximity to each other. Sitting in the chairs are eleven smiling friendly ex-drug addicts, all staring at me, like what I'm about to say carries the weight of the world.

"I was an angry bitter man," I say, smiling. "I thought everyone was an asshole. I was mean. Every time I looked in the mirror I really despised what I saw. I could see the faces of all the people I hurt. However, I didn't care. I just continued to hurt people. All that mattered was more and more and more. I owed a lot of bad people money. I thank God I'm not dead. I ended up...."

ONE YEAR EARLIER.

My eyes open. *What happened? Where am I? Fuck,* I blacked out. Again.

I try to recall what happened.

I was hanging out with Derek Defect in the Boston Commons, sitting by the statue, passing back and forth a Nalgene bottle filled with cheap wine. Two wiggers came strolling by, trying to start a fight with us. I wasn't surprised. They must've mistaken me for a Nazi, wearing a dirty white T-shirt with a swastika drawn in the center, with a Sharpie. I hate, but I'm not a Nazi. Everyone sucks!

We started out in Harvard Square, like always, then hopped on the train, riding it to Park St., where we bought a box of wine, filled up my Nalgene bottle so the wine was disguised from the cops, and drank at the Commons, sharing war stories; he talked about his band, and I talked about my girlfriend Scum Cunt.

So, two wiggers came by, thought I was a Nazi. Derek revealed a retractable steal baton from the inside pocket of his biker jacket, opening it with the flick of his wrist; I opened my stiletto switchblade. Derek swung his baton at the curly-haired wigger, who dodged it by diving head first into the statue. We both laughed. It was hysterical. I mean, the fucker was about to get brain-damaged by the baton, but instead he did it to himself.

The wiggers walked away, and we drank more wine, and now I'm here.

People are gathered around me, all standing, holding red plastic cups of beer, talking ... nonsense foaming at their mouths.

This party's making me sick-to-boot. Everyone's having a good time, except me. I'm a fish out of water.

The lights are dim. The walls are white and bland.

And the noise. The stereo's blasting what sounds like the mating rituals of a thousand dolphins on helium, and in the background's a chainsaw buzzing in slow motion, mixed with an obnoxious pounding, like someone pounding on my door when I just want to be left alone, shotgun blasts and glass shattering over and over again.

My head pulsates. My stomach churns. *Oh shit*, something's coming up.

Quickly, I stagger to the bathroom. I slam the door open. A girl is looking in the mirror, fixing her makeup. I shove her out of the way as I hurry to the toilet. I reach down and grab the sides of the toilet bowl. Holding tight, I plunge to my knees. My head almost drops in the bowl. Here it comes: an assortment of food and fluids mashed together to make a stew of vile sprays into the toilet, and it feels as if the rotten discharge is ripping up my insides on its way out, my stomach flipping outside-in; a few more heavy breaths and another round of retched spray pushes past my jugular and joins the rotten turbulent rollers bathing in the toilet bowl; then I upchuck chunks mixed with stomach acid that singes my throat even more so this time, leaving behind a rotten taste like that of expired cough syrup.

I stand up, grimacing, and wipe off my mouth.

I dolefully close the bathroom door, then look left. In front of me I see a stranger glaring at me. My eyes and his eyes meet. I don't like what I see, but I can*not* look away. I gaze desperately into the mirror, observing the stranger watch me, like coming face to face with my evil twin. The stranger is identical to me yet different in every way, mimicking my every move. I despise what I see. Like a donkey show—so intriguingly disgusting that I can't look away—my eyes are fixated on his. But I can't stand looking into the eyes of this sad sad *sad* excuse of a human being any longer.

Stop.

My right hand makes a fist. I swing my arm, my fist clashing with the mirror. An explosion. Shards of glass everywhere. The glass falls to the floor. I fall to the floor. Tears fall from my eyes. *Who am I? What have I become? A monster. A fiend?*

The door opens gently, and the painfully wretched noise becomes louder and more unbearable for a slight moment. An angel steps in. *How did she know I was in here? My savior.* She closes the door behind her. For the first time I detect the awful smell, the smell of stale vomit rising from the toilet. Effortlessly, I reach in my pocket, pull out a cigarette, place it in my mouth, then light it, hoping to mask the smell. Sitting on the floor, I scan the girl from head to toe: her half-red half-black hair sticks straight up, molded into spikes, like those of the Statue of Liberty, though each spike is randomly placed, covering her entire head; a leather dog collar, with six one-inch-long spikes poking out the front, is wrapped around her neck; a sleeveless white shirt with two lumps close to her collar covers her upper body; a pyramid-studded leather belt is fastened to her waist, wrapped through her belt loops, for style rather than necessity; a skintight black jean miniskirt squeezes her waist, and squeezing her legs are black fishnet tights tucked inside her Doctor Martin boots; she stands at about five feet and is agreeably thin.

She descends to her knees, picks up a shard of the mirror, and lays it between us. Unaffected by the smell, she looks at me and smiles. I awkwardly force a smile, tears still dripping down my face, as I avoid eye contact with her.

She digs through her pocket to present a plastic bag filled with white powder. I see the powder. My eyes widen with anticipation. I'm suddenly excited, my heart racing. My hands tremble. The phenomenal thought of being high makes me high. *Hurry up!*

Still teary-eyed, I look at her. She looks at me, sprinkling the contents of the bag onto the mirror shard. I remember last winter. *The snow falling.* I remember the late nights last winter when I waited in the freezing cold outside of McDonald's after they'd closed, waiting for my fix. *Was it worth it? It was like listening to a girl's bullshit only because she sucks a mean dick. Some nights were better than others. Sometimes one has to go through hell to get what one wants. Why do people work? Why do anything dreadful, for that matter? The light at the end of the tunnel. The more shit I put up with, the brighter the light, the better the climax. Sucking down that crack pipe took care of the cold, instantly warming me up, and the colder I was, the warmer I felt. I felt like I earned it, like having a cold beer after a long day at work.*

The angel retrieves her wallet from her back pocket. She slips her credit card out of her wallet. I watch. With her credit card she shapes the powder into two crisp white lines. I wait. She hands me a rolled one-dollar bill.

Holding one end of the tube in my right nostril, pinching my left nostril closed, I touch the mirror with the dollar bill. Moving the tube along one fine white line, I sniff powerfully.

A jolt of white lightning straight to my brain. I feel revived, like waking up from a wet dream.

My savior.

The tears in my eyes. Oh yes, the tears in my eyes, they have evaporated. Gone. No more. I am alive. I am the king of the world. I can do anything, anything, anything I want. Nothing can stop me now. I feel godly. I feel fucking superb. *This is better than any sex.* Everything appears brighter and much more vibrant, much more real ... surreal, out of this world. My senses enhance. I touch the girl's face. Her smooth skin sends shivers down my spine. My whole body's numb. My thoughts come to a complete stop. Then speed up, like a reverse half-life, doubling in speed, getting faster ... *BRAIN* ... and ... *DEAD* ... faster ... and ... faster ... and ... faster ... and faster ... and faster ... faster ... faster ... faster, faster, faster faster fasterfaster-festaroutrstefoffetsracontroltsefar. I glance at the angel as she sucks her line through her nose. We both stand up. Slamming the girl into the wall, I grab the back of her head, pushing her face into mine, gorging on her spit.

I wrap my arms around her. I move my hands up and down, rubbing her back. I squeeze her ass. *Soft but firm. The way I like it.* Then it hits me. *Her fucking wallet.* The sly cunt I am, I slip my fingers into her back pocket, liberating her wallet, then I carefully place it in my right side pocket.

She drops to her knees, unbuttons and unzips my pants, then pulls out my cock. *I don't* need *her; I feel good enough as it is, but I* want *her ... I want her badly.*

After fifteen to twenty minutes of sucking, fondling, jerking, blowing, licking, and spitting, I grab her head, slide her off my cock, jerk my shaft twice, blow a load all over her face, then continue to pump my cock like a Super Soaker, discharging more spurts, each blast carrying a little less come. When I finish emptying my balls all over the slut's face, I grab her head again and throw her to the bathroom floor. *Oh, FUCK, I've got to get more. The cocaine was fucking supreme, but I need more, NOW*. I hear a voice say, "You fucking asshole, I cut myself on the glass," but I ignore it. I leave the bathroom and the party. Down the stairs, out the front door, hitting the city streets, where I discover forty-six dollars in the cunt's wallet. *Nice catch.*

I pull my phone out of my pocket. I call Adam. I call Tim. I call Laura. Nobody answers. *Fuck. Maybe I ought to call Lenny. No, I owe him sixty dollars. Yes*? *No*? *Yes.* I call Lenny.

Ring, ring! Ring, ring!

"Hello?" Lenny says tiredly.

"It's Bradley."

"What do you want, Brad?"

"Can I get a forty-bag?"

"You still owe me sixty!"

"I'm going to get the money tonight. I swear."

"Hard or soft?" he asks dismissively.

"Hard."

"You better get me that fucking money." He hangs up.

I'm going to get some crack, I'm going to get some crack, I sing silently as I skip toward Lenny's apartment, feeling better already. I'm mad with excitement. I'm insane.

I ring Lenny's doorbell. "I'll be right there," I hear him yell.

I wait outside, bored, wondering, *What the fuck's taking so long?* for close to ten minutes.

Lenny opens the door, gesturing for me to come in. I take two steps through his door, and, *fuck me*, he throws me to the ground, enraged. *What the fuck's his problem?*

Pointing a gun at me, "I will kill you," Lenny warns, "if I do not see my money by twelve-o'clock tomorrow."

Nervously and slowly, and slightly frightened, I nod my head in agreement.

Standing beside me, Lenny throws down a small bag with what looks like crystals inside. *Who does this cunt think I am?* I pick up the bag and leave.

I guess I need to make sixty dollars by tomorrow. I walk two blocks and see an alley to my left. *This place will do*. I creep down the alley and crouch behind a dumpster. I pull my pipe out of my pocket, then place a rock on the end. I hold the pipe vertically, facing upwards, light it, then suck. ....So gratifying. M-m-my thoughts stutter. My whole body's quivering. I've just woken up from a deep sleep. I take another hit. *Silence*.

I've just gracefully killed twenty minutes. *Why do I do this to myself?*

I hit the street. I need to find a sucker. I go to the park. *Fuck, I don't feel so good.* In every inch of my body my nerves scream out for more. I feel like crawling out of my skin. Sweat leaks out of my pores, like a wet rag being squeezed in a vice.

I sit down on a park bench, pull out my pipe, place a rock on the end, light it, and my nerves are settled. Another hit. *Right on the spot*. The sky, it's beautiful. The stars ... so shiny. I'm overly comfortable. *This bench is the place to be*. I switch from sitting to lying down. I can lay here forever, or at least until my high wears down, which is right now, and the anxiety attacks me again. I sit up, then hang my head, curling into the fetal position. *Don't panic, don't panic,* I think as I rock back and forth uncomfortably.

I see a guy in a black suit coming toward me. He gets closer as I hide behind a tree. He gets closer, and closer and closer.

I step out from behind the tree and then grab the man's collar, pulling him toward me. "GIMME YOUR FUCKIN' MONEY!" I scream, pointing my knife at his neck.

The man remains silent, completely still, just staring at me.

"I said, gimme your money!"

"Okay, okay. Here, it's yours." He pulls out a wad of cash held together with a money clip, then hands it to me.

I take the cash and run.

I exit the park. Standing on the sidewalk, bent over, I breathe heavily. In the distance, sirens wail, increasing in volume, getting closer. I perform a steady jog.

"Hey, you. Stop!" a voice from behind me yells.

I speed up. I hear boots beating the pavement, sounding like a modest drum roll. I look back. A short chubby middle-aged police officer is gaining on me. The drumroll gets louder and *louder* and *LOUDER* and ***LOUDER!*** and....

ONE YEAR LATER.

"I ended up in cuffs," I conclude, "behind bars, with nothing. I thought everyone was an asshole. Now I realize I was the asshole. Getting arrested one year ago was a blessing in disguise, because I have not used drugs since. Thank you."

"THANKS, BRADLEY!" eleven addicts chant.

Not a Pretty Picture

A short story....

"... Amanda sprayed with the steaming water from the blast: stinging her skin ..."

AMANDA AWAKING FROM A DREADFUL dream ... sitting up in bed ... startled ... the breathing walls inflating and deflating ... inflating and deflating: all four walls ... not right, she can tell ... sweat streaming down her face ... Amanda rubbing the sweat out of her eyes ... taking another look: the walls ... *purple!* ... not her room ... her walls: white ... with band posters ... Amanda wanting to roll out of bed ... but the floor: a bright orange ... moving ... flowing; a river, molten lava ... small orange bubbles growing ... inflating ... becoming transparent: *pop!* ... steam wafting out ... Amanda gripping the covers ... pulling them over her head ... counting: *one two three four five six seven eight nine ten* ... removing the covers: the blue walls bleeding ... splattered blood beating from the ceiling ... Amanda looking up at the source: a blinding light beaming into her eyes; a vengeance ... so bright: Amanda having to snap her eyes shut ... and still: even with her eyes shut ... even in the darkness ... blue polka dots popping up ... then red ... green ... Amanda opening her eyes ... in a giant bubble ... floating up: the pink sky ... around her: other girls in bubbles floating up ... Amanda trying to scream ... all that comes out:

three frivolously floating bubbles ... *pop!* one two three ... Amanda finally standing up ... needing a better view of her whereabouts ... but while standing: the big bubble bursts ... Amanda falling ... screaming ... flailing her arms and legs ... her stomach flip-flopping ... flip-flopping ... her plaid pajamas fluttering ... the pink sky darkening ... Amanda plunging deeper ... deeper ... deeper ... darkness: all she can see ... Amanda clasping her hands together ... still falling ... praying: "Please God please God please God help me help me *HELP ME*" ... her flailing body surging into cold water ... the pressure trying to push her back up ... Amanda sinking deeper ... deeper: light entering the darkness ... the bleak water steadily becoming bluer: a lighter shade of blue ... Amanda drifting downward ... surfacing ... stranded in the ocean ... floating ... her eyes scanning the abyss: cannot see any signs of life ... none ... the sea: miles and miles ... every direction ... Amanda flapping her arms: little ripples of waves forming from her fingertips ... Amanda turning: one-hundred-eighty degrees ... the bleak blue sky blanketing the bleak blue abyss: miles and miles ... the sea as still as the sky: no waves ... no wind ... Amanda yelling: "Anybody out there!" ... no answer ... then an unfamiliar feeling: sharp pricks; an inside-out porcupine ... flashing through her ... followed by a total numbness ... Amanda shaking spasmodically; tremors ... a sickening fear ... *what is happening to me?* ... Amanda turning again: one-hundred-eighty degrees ... still nothing ... *where am I?* Amanda wanting to know ... her fluttering body becoming still ... as still as the wind ... and the water ... Amanda hearing something ... something ... anything ... a sound ... *her savior* ... yes? ... no ... her imagination ... then: the wet water no longer wet ... but dry: very very dry ... in fact: dry*ing* ... warm air; a blow dryer ... *strange* ... Amanda still floating in the water ... but drying off ... *very strange* ... the sun falling fast: fast ... splashing into the water; a big brick ... Amanda sprayed with the steaming water from the blast: *stinging her skin* ... darkness descending upon her ... the waves picking up ... blasting her in the face ... the wind blowing ... rattling the waving water: the swirling rapids ... Amanda: scared ... oh so very scared ... she cannot see the waves: but feels them ... the violent bursts of wind knocking her around ... Amanda turning ... turning ... twisting ... tumbling ... the bold waves getting a crushing grip on her ... pulling her under ... pushing her over: over ... under ... over ... under ... over and over again ... Amanda: lost at sea ... knowing not which way is up nor down ... twisting ... turning ... twisting ... turning ... flailing; a fish out of water ... waving with the waves: over ... under ... over ... under ... over and over again ... over and over again ... over and over again!!!

A big tiger ... black and orange stripes ... lunging at her ... pushing her backwards ... pinning her to the sand ... a desert ... no more water ... warm air ... hot air ... a big tongue slipping out of the grinning tiger ... swabbing her face ... Amanda squirming ... trying to break lose ... no escape ... the tiger: too strong ... much too strong ... the tiger's tongue caressing her face: grimacing ... disgusted ... a snake slithering past her head ... sounding like a grilling hamburger ... sizzling ... slithering past her torso, her legs ... the snake: eight inches ... the tiger's wet tongue still slapping her in the face ... the bright yellow sun burning her bare skin ... the snake forming a U by her foot ... turning around ... sidling beside her pale leg, into her plaid pajamas

... Amanda still squirming ... trying to break free from the tiger's tight grip ... sensing the slithering snake slipping up her bare leg: tickling her skin ... haunted thoughts meandering in her mind ... Amanda letting loose a glass-shattering shriek ... screaming bloody murder as the snake stops still ... the tiger's tongue slipping back into its mouth ... its awful grin growing ... stretching out ... smiling: a psychotic smile; that of a killer before cutting your throat ... then: a piercing pain penetrating her flesh ... digging deep ... stabbing her back; a knife ... ripped out ... stabbing again ... rapid stabbing ... in and out ... in and out ... tears falling from her eyes ... the tiger's warm breath blowing in her face: rotten fish ... Amanda closing her eyes ... praying again ... silently ... *please God please God please God help me help me HELP ME* ... the searing pain suddenly stopping ... *thank God* ... the tiger dismounting her ... crawling backwards ... backwards ... Amanda sitting up ... leaning on her elbows: perched in the sand ... the hot sand ... Amanda watching: the tiger traipsing in a circle ... a full circle: three-hundred-sixty degrees ... staring at Amanda ... grinning ... words slipping out of the tainted tiger's mouth, through its tainted teeth: "Amanda, wake up! ... wake up, Amanda!" ... a deep growl ... "wake up! ... wake up, Amanda!"

Her eyes open to her dim-lit bedroom, a familiar face hovering over her.

"Amanda" ... shaking her!

Her father? ... no, her stepfather!

"Amanda, you were having a bad dream. You were screaming. But it's over, Amanda, it's over."

Her rapid breathing slows to a steady inhale ... exhale ... sweet sweet relief, that's how she feels: relieved ... but tired, worn out, ready to fall back asleep. She closes her eyes, and her stepfather presses his wet lips against her forehead ... a sweet succulent kiss ... before he slips off the bed and leaves the room. Then Amanda cascades into a posttraumatic slumber....

R.I.P.
William Taylor, 1997

A short story....

"... not a word spoken as they delved downstairs, four black briefcases dangling from four left hands ..."

I

HELLO, MY NAME IS BOBBY Taylor, thirty-two-years old, married to a beautiful Chinese woman named Mia, and we have a six-year-old son, Billy, named after my twin brother, Will, who passed away when we were ten. Billy is the second most important person in my life, Mia being the first, of course. Mia and I have a baby girl on the way, whom we are thinking about naming Christina, although, personally, I like the name Jacky. We have a wonderful Australian Shepard named Trader. Mia, Billy, Trader, and I all live in Miami Beach, Florida, in a big house—unnecessarily big, I suppose—overlooking the beach. One could say we are rich, but I would prefer to say we are well off. I write for a living, particularly ghost stories based upon nightmares I have had. The book that has paid for this house is called *I Dream of Ghosts*. We have made a fortune after a big-time Hollywood producer, Al ------- (he has asked that I do not use his last name), turned *I Dream of Ghosts* into a major motion picture starring Christian Bale.

Anyway, this story I am about to tell you is not about me, as much as you would expect it to be. No, it is about William Taylor, my twin brother.

Margery Moran and Eugene Taylor had fallen deeply in love and married only one year after they had met, Margery already pregnant. Mom was three months into her pregnancy, carrying Will and myself, when she and Dad had eloped. I say "eloped" only because Mom's parents were against the wedding, although Dad's parents, Nana and Papa, were for it and encouraged it to go on—they simply adored Mom, treated her like one of their own. Mom's parents, however, had disowned her because Dad was, and still is, an alcoholic, only today he is a recovering alcoholic.

So, they had married in the year 1987, and six months later a cute little boy whom they would name William Taylor was born. Exactly two hours and twenty-three minutes later I was born and they would name me Bobby Taylor. From then on, Will and I were inseparable. We would go on to do just about everything together.

Mom, Dad, Will, and I lived, during our first year together, in a small two-family house—the right side was ours—of which I have no recollection because I was so young. A year later, after Dad had gotten a major promotion, we moved to a big house—well, a decent size compared to my current abode—in a suburbs of Boston, MA, known as Newton. Newton is technically a city and urban, but we lived in a suburban-like town of Newton called Oak Hill Park.

This is what I remember about our house—the house I grew up in: It was a blue three-decker house, sandwiched between two similar-looking houses, although the neighboring houses were painted beige. (The neighbors, Dad would say, were upset with us after he had painted the house blue, but Dad was never a fan of conformity, had always liked to stand out in some way or the other—he would wear flamboyant ties to work, which was allowed since he was the boss—because, I am assuming, his family was a military family, and he had grown up on a military base, and uniformity must have been everything to them. Again, this is only speculation, so do not quote me on it.) However, Dad had a "keeping up with the Joneses" style to him too. Our front yard was always well groomed. And the back mirrored the front, only there was a big tree in the center, leaning a little to the right, upon which a dilapidated tree house had been built by the previous owners—but Dad had fixed it up, made it safe for Will and I to play in—with large branches weaving in and out of the windows. (Boy, did I love that tree house. We had so much fun in there. On weekends Will and I would camp out in it and stay up all night and play card games and board games.) A white picket fence surrounded our backyard, keeping the neighbors out. (I remember Dad would fight with this one neighbor, Pete I think his name was, because a large maple tree in *his* backyard loomed over the fence, invading *our* property, and Dad wanted it removed, but Pete would not budge. They would argue constantly.) So, that was the outside.

When you would walk in the front door, you would come across the entryway, a little square room with a coat closet to your right and a bench under which shoes were planted to your left. Still in the entryway with your back against the door, you would be looking at a stairway leading up to the second floor, and parallel to the stairway on the left side was a short hall leading to the kitchen. Then to the left of the short hall was the dining room. To the right of the stairway was the living room. So if you were standing with your back to the front door you would have four options—walk up the stairs, walk through the short hall, take a left into the dining room, or take a right into the living room. Both the living room and the dining room would also take you to the kitchen. A bathroom branched off the kitchen and a TV room branched off the living room.

Then there was the second floor. Directly at the top of the stairs was a bathroom. Then after two lefts you would be in a hallway that passed my old bedroom, which Will and I had shared, and would take you to my parents' master bedroom, which had its own private master bathroom. That was the house I grew up in.

But there was a third floor too, which was off limits to the two of us, stimulating curiosity of the worst degree—curiosity killed the cat. On the right side of the house was an outside staircase that rose above the second floor and stopped at a door, the only entrance to the forbidden third floor. Speculation ran wild between us. We would tell ghost stories about the third floor when we camped out in our tree house. Sometimes when we were all sitting around the dining room table eating dinner I would ask: "What's up in the third floor?" and Dad would say: "You'll understand when you're older," or, "Nothing for you to worry about." Otherwise, nobody would mention anything about it, like it did not exist.

In the summer of 1994, when I was seven-years old, I had seen Dad and three other men exit the third floor; Will and I camped out in the tree house. Will would always fall asleep with ease, but I struggled to sleep. Always had. I take Trauzadone to help with that every night. As Will slept like a baby, snoring serenely, I heard the squeaking of a rusty doorknob, and the sound stole my attention. I gazed out the tree house's window when the door to the third floor barged open, a bright green light spilling out onto the landing. Four black silhouettes stepped out silently, and the door shut as they descended the staircase, not a word spoken as they delved downstairs, four black briefcases dangling from four left hands. My eyes followed them the whole way down. I could see that Dad had worn a black tie, matching his black suit, which was strange because he would never—and I mean *never*—be caught dead wearing a "normal" matching tie. They had all worn black suit-and-tie getups and black fedoras, I noticed as they entered their three black Sedans, parked in the driveway, under the glint of the glowing streetlights. Their engines released a muffled roar, and they all drove away in different directions as Dad was nowhere to be seen, probably entering the house, which was around the corner—thus out of my line of sight.

II

THIS STORY, THE MADNESS, ALL began one hot summer day when Dad was at work and Mom and Michelle were upstairs in bed with a bad case of the flu. We were eight years old and left alone for the first time ever.

We were sitting cross-legged on the floor of the tree house playing Checkers when I asked Will: "Do you ever think about *actually* going up to the third floor? I mean, to just look around, to see what's up there?"

"That's silly, the third floor is off limits. You know that."

"But our parents are—"

"Bobby, don't be stupid. Anyway, it's your move."

Like always, I was red and he was black.

"We goof about the third floor all the time," I said, "and you're telling me you've *never* even thought about going up there?"

"I've *thought* about it, but I would never *actually* go through with it."

"Why not?"

"I guess I'm a chicken."

"But I wanna go up there," I said, "and I can't go alone."

"Why not? You're a big boy."

"Call me a chicken too. *Please* will you go with me?"

"I'm not—"

"Please?"

"If it will get you to shut up, then yes."

"Thank you, Will." I lunged over the Checkers board and hugged Will. At that moment he made me so happy. I was proud to call him my brother.

After we had picked up the Checkers pieces and board, stored them in the Checkers box, we climbed down the ladder of the tree house, ventured to the dreaded staircase.

At the bottom of the stairs, both of us peering upward, anxiety sifting through our blood, hearts beating inconsistently, Will said: "Are you sure you wanna do this?"

"Yes, Will, I do," I replied sternly, not about to back down. No way! This was my idea and I would go through with it no matter what.

We stood there staring at the hike we would have to make, petrified—or at least I was petrified, although I would never admit it. A minute passed as our wide eyes investigated the only way up, readying our childish courage.

"Any minute now," said Will.

"I'm scared." I wanted to change my mind then. This was too much. I was only eight.

"This was your idea. Come on." Will stepped up to the plate and started up the staircase, with me following behind. The unused wooden steps creaked as we ascended upward. We could hear the old rusty wood crying beneath our feet, like an old wooden door opening and closing. With every step the wood moaned as if it had feelings, as if it were in pain.

A quarter of the way up I said finally: "Maybe we shouldn't." With my mind almost made, I stood behind Will, arms folded.

"This was your idea," Will snapped—and I had never seen him act like he was acting today—"Come on!" He was acting possessed.

I followed Will three steps behind. He was overcome with confidence, it seemed. What happened to *"I guess I'm a chicken"*? Will did not seem to be the least bit chicken. He stopped halfway up on the landing, level with the second floor.

"Do you hear that?" asked Will.

"Hear what?"

"That."

"I hear nothing."

"Come here."

I climbed the three steps dividing Will and myself and entered the landing. Now I stood trembling on the landing, and I heard it. I could not make sense of what I heard. I would try to explain, but any attempt at articulating the sound would only come across as gibberish. Nothing could describe the awful sound coming from the dreaded third floor. I would use metaphors or similes, but this sound was like nothing I had heard before. Nothing.

BANG!!!

I heard a hammer banging an upside-down steel trashcan—*bang, bang, bang!!!* Then a scurrying sound, like rats stampeding across the floor.

BANG!!!—I heard it again. Glass shattering.

It did not make any sense. Only three steps below where I stood, I had heard nothing, but here and now I could hear a whole ensemble of noises. Like an orchestra using household items. And the scurrying I am sure was only rats. But what made the other sounds? And that initial indescribable sound I had heard?

We stood holding hands, trembling violently.

Will asked: "Are you ready?"

"Ready for what?" I forgot the purpose of us being here. Was there a purpose?

"To go."

"I'm too scared," I uttered, slightly embarrassed.

"I'm ready." He spoke, but not to me. There was something else.

Will stepped up slowly as I stood watching. He was really doing it. The sounds echoed in my skull—*bang, bang, bang!!!* I decided that if I was going to stay here, I would take three steps back to escape the harsh sounds thrashing in my ears. So I turned, descended three steps, turned again, watched as Will entered the forbidden door leading to the third floor. Silence was all I could hear. Thank God. I waited for some time. I did not know how long I waited because I had no watch, but I can assure you it was a long time. Then:

"Aaaaaaaaaaaaaaahhhhhhhhhhh!!!" A horrific howl hailed from the third floor. It was Will. I was too much of a chicken to rescue him. I did what most eight-year olds would do. I ran away. In the opposite direction. Descended the stairs. Entered the house. I needed to tell Mom, and—

In the kitchen Will was making a peanut-butter-and-jelly sandwich.

"Wha ... wha ... wha ..."

He looked at me.

"You ... you ... you were just upstairs."

"Yea, and I came down here to make a sandwich. So what?"

"Wha ... wha ... what happened?"

"Are you okay, Bobby?"

III

AFTER THAT DAY WILL HAD begun acting strange. He started wearing his shoes on the wrong feet and his clothes backwards. Nobody found this odd, but me. Will had always been nitpicky when it came to clothing. He could never wear anything dirty. Not only that but wearing clothes lopsided always caused him complete confusion. It would always set him off in a very bad way. In our bedroom there were a few pictures of Will and me, and I would always turn the pictures slightly askew just to watch him squirm. Do not forget, even though we loved each other dearly, we were brothers first, and yes, I liked to toy with Will's weaknesses.

Then came the vomiting. He could not hold down his food. Mom tried cooking him soups and toast, but it would all come up like everything else he would eat. So they brought him to the doctor, and he was diagnosed with a brain tumor. It was a sad day for all of us.

Things had kept getting worse for poor Will. He would get confused over the smallest tasks. He had to be pushed in a wheelchair because he would at times forget how to walk. He would sometimes hurt himself really badly: a few fractured ribs, a broken arm, a fractured kneecap, a concussion.

By the time he had turned nine he already forgot my name. Mom, he would call "Dad," and Dad, he would call "Mom." Everything was messed up in his mind. I felt awful, for it was my idea to venture up to the third floor. I started seeing a shrink after Mom had found me beating my head against a wall. I wanted to die. Our whole family had been turned upside-down ever since the diagnosis. Dad was yelling all the time and Mom was crying. Michelle was forgotten about and sent to a foster home. Our family was screwed up, and it was all my fault.

Then Will had died at the age of ten in 1997. Poor poor Will. I had never even thought about the third floor after that. It was as if any thought of the horrid third floor had vanished from my mind, as if it had never really existed and this was all just my imagination and so was Will, my imagination.

IV

IT WAS TWO YEARS AGO, when I was thirty, twenty years after Will had passed, when weird occurrences started to take place in *my* once ordinary life, when I could remember again, remember the horror. I had just gotten out of the shower when it happened. I wrapped a blue towel, which had been hanging on the bathroom door, around my soaking wet waste. I turned to look in the mirror, which was above the sink, and opened it, behind where I found four small shelves, the top two lined with medicine bottles, the bottom shelve holding my toothbrush and dental floss, and one shelf above was a fingernail clipper, toenail clipper, and comb. My toothpaste was perched on the left corner of the sink, and my mouthwash the right corner. I reached for my toothbrush, which lay flat on the bottom shelf, and gripped it between thumb, pointer, and middle finger. Then when I closed the mirror I saw Will in the reflection sitting behind me on the tub. I turned the sink faucets, mixing hot water with cold, allowing a warm flow of water to splash in the sink and slip down the drain—*shshshshshshshsh*—testing the temperature with my hand, experimenting, until I concocted the perfect mix of hot and cold. When the water was warm, but not too warm, I applied toothpaste to my toothbrush, and—

Will was sitting behind me on the tub.

I jumped, halted, turned, focused, and the bathroom was empty. It must have been my imagination. I turned around and gazed deeply in the mirror. I was pale as a ghost, soaked, hair flattened to my head, water running down my face, like a long-distance runner after a marathon. I investigated my toothbrush, then spotted the thick pink paste, which looked like bubble gum, on the white tile floor. The toothpaste, I assumed, must have flown from my brush as I had reacted so abruptly to ... to ... to my own mind's treacherous trick. I grabbed a piece of paper towel, ripped it from the roll, accidentally glanced quickly in the mirror, and Will was sitting behind me on the tub, I noticed through the corner of my eye, did a double-take, and Will was nowhere to be found. I resumed. I dropped to my hands and knees, wiped up the toothpaste, stood, saw that Will was sitting behind me on the tub, my jaw dropped, and stunned by what I was seeing, I slowly took a step back, eyes bulging out in horror. I could see Will as clear as day. He looked exactly like he did before he had passed, wearing the same black suit he had worn in the coffin, the suit he was buried in. I could not believe my eyes. Feet planted firmly in place, I peered over my shoulder, and no one was sitting on the tub. I gazed in the mirror again, and I could see Will behind me, not blinking, as if lazar-beams were zipping from his eyes straight into mine, soul-searching, like I was making a clairvoyant connection. I was creeped out at first, but then kind of ignored him as I proceeded to brush my teeth, floss, gulp a mouthful of mouthwash, swish, spit, and leave the bathroom swiftly, slipping through the door. If the truth be told, I did not really believe what I had seen. I mean, how could I? Will was dead, died, passed away, and I would have been ca-ca-ca-crazy, completely psychotic, if I had surrendered, given in, to my mind's tomfoolery without a fight.

In the past two years leading up to today, I had seen Will a few other times appearing in various ways. I had seen him lying in bed next to Mia through my bedroom mirror. I had seen him sitting to the right of Billy in the backseat of my car through the rearview mirror. And, last but not least, I had seen him walk out in front of my car when I was stuck in bumper-to-bumper traffic completely still.

V

SO, THAT IS MY STORY—well, Will's story, actually—and it is about time I put an end to the torment, to the pain, to the dreams, to the nightmares, and face my fears.

Now, standing at the bottom of the outside staircase, my right foot planted firmly on the first step, knees bent, my right hand gripping the railing, a strong tight nervous grip, my left hand flat on the wall, pressing powerfully, like a downhill skier at the starting post, gripping the rails on both sides, ready to push off; my head hung down, eyes fixed on my feet, heart beating nervously, I raise my head, gazing up to the top, gawking, sweat beating down my face. I have to put an end to this madness, and what better time than now, at Will's twenty-two-year anniversary of the day he passed away—the whole family, Mom and Dad and Michelle and her husband and Billy and Trader and Mia, who is pregnant with Christina, and cousins and aunts and uncles, everyone who was familiar with William Taylor, have gathered for the event, standing around inside, talking with one another, and I have excused myself to use the bathroom, a white lie I have told to ensure that no one tries to stop me, because I am destined to put the puzzle in order, even if it kills me. I lift my left foot passed my right, dropping it down on the second step. I stop. *Come on, you can do it,* I tell myself, and then start up the steps as the wood cries out like a pissed off cat. I bite my bottom lip at the sound. A loud bass drum is kicked, and I stop again, realizing it was only thunder when a bright yellow flash lights up the gray cloudy sky. This is too much. But I start up again, slowly. A single scared tear falls from my right eye. I stop, catch my heavy breath, before I start again, panting, as if I have just been held under water. Okay, I can do this. I have to. A quarter of the way up, a loud explosion thunders, and I jump, startled by the sound, before the sky lights up fast, a brief yellow flash. The steps continue to scream in pain as I ascend upward. I finally lift my feet onto the landing, level with the second floor, and a sound unlike any I have heard before—*here we go again*—echoes loudly in my skull—*bang, bang, bang!!!* Scurrying, banging, shattering, dinging, screaming sounds stop suddenly, so that silence is all I can hear, and then:

Bobby! Will's voice, the same as I remember it. I did not hear it, but rather sensed it, like in a dream. *Come on up, Bobby! I've been waiting for you!* I am starting to think twice about traveling the rest of the way up. This is not going to end well. Cannot end well. I turn, about to descend the stairs when I feel something, like a noose around my neck, tugging at me. Pulling me. I feel compelled to finish what I have started. I cannot finish it, though. There is no end. I take one step down, then another step, a third step, turn, then I start back up. I have to reach the top, see what is up there. I just have to. I cannot explain why.

"Bobby!" It is Mia, calling me from the bottom. "What are you doing up there?!"

I look down at her, open my mouth, try to speak, but something is caught in my throat and I cannot make out a single word. Something strange is happening here, and I cannot put my finger on it. I have to finish this, put it to an end. Another burst of thunder thrashes in the sky, and in an instant later rain begins to fall heavily.

"Bobby!" Mia shouts. "I said, what are you doing up there?! You're going to catch a cold! Come down here, NOW!!!"

The sky darkens, and a thunderous bang roars fiercely as a bright yellow zigzag cuts the sky in half. There is no turning back. I am in this for the long haul. Mia catches my gaze, and she starts up the steps.

"Noooooooo!!!" I scream. "Don't come up here! This is something I have to face alone!"

I start again, a steady gaze focused on the top, and the loud thrashing, smashing, crashing, bashing begins, this time louder and louder, gaining in volume as I get closer to my destination. I look over my shoulder, and Mia is joining me, apparently, so I turn, hold out my hand, signaling her to stop.

"Mia, please. Don't come any farther."

"Bobby," Mia says. "What is going on?"

"I'll explain later. Please."

She stops where she is, and I turn back around, now facing the top. I stand still for a moment, catching my breath as the painful pounding beats my brain. I start moving again, faster than before, as if it is a race.

At the top of the stairs I twist the door handle clockwise. Then when I crack the door the sounds switch off as if the door has flipped a switch. I continue to crack the door farther open, and I am hit with a bright green light, too bright to make out clearly what is inside, only that there are objects in the room silhouetted against the light. When I let go of the handle it turns counterclockwise fast on its own, snapping back into place.

"Bobby!" Mia calls.

I divert my gaze to the staircase, and Mia is standing a quarter of the way up—and I am glad she is there as opposе to halfway up, tormented by the terrifying noise—watching me.

"Bobby!" she repeats.

"Mia, everything will be fine; just don't come any farther. Please!"

I enter the green light, and I cannot see a single thing—well—except for a few silhouetted objects. The green light switches off—or should I say on? as I can see clearly now—and ...

I reach into the cupboard to fetch a jar of peanut butter when I hear:

"Wha ... wha ... wha ..."

It is Mia, and I look at her.

"You ..." she stammers. "You ... you were just upstairs."

"Are you okay, Mia?"

"Wha ... what happened?"

"What are you talking about? There's a party going on in the living room, what would I be doing up," I stop, think about what I am saying, then finish, "stairs?"

The Joke's on You

A short story....

"... ignoring him outa spite for his stupid suggestion, because Billy's great & Gregory's being a total buzz-kill, & then things start moving & the party's only picking up ..."

THE SCENE: It's Halloween night. I was just in Salem, MA, like every Halloween night since I was 11. I'm on my way home, riding in a car with Gregory, who's dressed like the Joker in *Batman*, driving. Gregory's costume resembles the Joker dead on. The time's a few minutes past 2 in the morning—OK, I lied: it's not Halloween anymore. The looming full moon shines bright thru the clouds that cover the dark sky. It looks like it might rain soon. The front windows are open halfway, mine & his. There's a cigarette wedged between my pointer & middle finger & the smoke is sucked out thru the open window. The wind's whacking me in the face, hard, but silently because Johnny Thunders & the Heartbreakers are playing on the stereo. The car's soaring above the speed limit, which is, I think, 60 miles per hour.

How fast are we going? I ask Gregory.

He says nothing. I forgot to mention we are really drunk, & I didn't think to turn down the volume before speaking. I twist the nob.

How fast are we going? I ask again.

The Joker looks at me & his creepy costume sends a shiver down my spine.

He says, *About 85.*

There you have it—we are driving at about 85 miles per hour.

THE STORY: In the distance, I point out to Gregory, there's a man—maybe my age, maybe older, maybe younger, who knows?—& he's walking backwards, with his right hand extended & his thumb sticking straight up, & as we get closer I can see he's wearing raggedy jeans & a long-sleeve flannel shirt, buttoned up. His hair's cut short.

Wanna pick him up? I say.

Gregory presses the brake pedal & turns the wheel right & we veer that way, merging with the breakdown lane, & I can see the hitchhiker's tan skin as he hops in the backseat & we're off, picking up speed, & the car settles at about 85 miles per hour again.

I'm Billy, says the hitchhiker.

I introduce myself & Gregory, who says:

Where to?

Billy tells us the name of a college not too far away while Johnny Thunders & the Heartbreakers continue to play quietly & I turn up the volume.

Thanks for picking me up, Billy says.

Why're you hitchhiking? I say.

This girl, Billy says. *She ditched me, took off with the car.*

That, I say. *That really sucks.*

Who are we listening to?

Johnny Thunders, I say, *& the Heartbreakers.*

You mean, like, Tom Petty & the Heartbreakers?

I grimace. *Fuck, no. This is JOHNNY THUNDERS & the Heartbreakers'* L.A.M.F.

What's L.A.M.F.*?*

That gets Gregory's attention & he looks at me fast, & it looks as though he's angry, fuckin pissed off, probably because he has a psychotic smile painted on his face, & that smile still doesn't sit right with me; it still makes me quiver. He looks back at the road.

I say, *Like a Motherfucker.*

Billy nods, then sits back in his seat.

We're moving along steadily, enjoying the tunes, & I'll tell you something else, I really like Billy's company, especially when he says:

I got 'shrooms.

With you? I ask, all giddy-like.

He shakes his head.

At my dorm, he says.

Gregory's not paying any attention.

I say to him, *He's got 'shrooms.*

I heard, says Gregory—& I guess he is paying attention.

Rain starts to pour, splashing on the windshield, & the windshield wipers wipe away the rain as more rain splashes down, & it looks like we're under a waterfall peering up thru a transparent umbrella, watching the water splatter against the see-through shield, & the car swerves every now & then, but I don't worry too much, because Gregory, a.k.a. the Joker, is usually a pretty decent driver when drunk.

We park in a big parking lot surrounding a big brick building & Gregory shuts off the engine & all 3 doors open simultaneously & we step out into the rain. Gregory & Billy hurry to the door as I pick up the steel pipe lying beside my seat (I carried the pipe with me all night because I'd decided to dress as a football hooligan for Halloween), then slam the door shut & rush to catch up, running thru the door Billy's holding open. He closes the door after I go thru. Billy leads the way & we follow & I knock on every door we pass & Gregory tells me to stop, but I don't listen, just *knock-knock-knock* the whole way to Billy's room. Billy's laughing though; he finds it funny.

We stop at a door & Billy inserts his key, twists it, opens the door, & gestures for us to go in & Gregory goes thru first, followed by me, & we're in what looks like a common room & I hear the door shut behind me. There are a few doors, one of which is wide open & I can see right thru, & a guy sitting on the couch in front of us cranes his head & is looking at me, staring, gawking, & I meet his gaze, gawking right back.

This is Jeremy, says Billy, gesturing to the guy on the couch.

He then gives him our names, mine & Gregory's, & Jeremy doesn't say anything, just cranes his head back at the wide-screen TV in front of him.

Wait right here, Billy says.

I sit down on the couch beside Jeremy while Gregory's doing something, I don't know what, looking for something, I suppose.

What're you watching? I say to Jeremy.

He doesn't speak. He doesn't even look at me, doesn't even acknowledge me. I wanna smack him, break his jaw, though I'm waiting for the 'shrooms & I don't wanna fuck that up. Billy comes back into the room & hands me a bag filled with mushrooms. I open the bag & remove a handful, then stuff them in my mouth & they taste very bland, very dry, like cardboard, & I chew them up before swallowing.

I pass the bag to Gregory & he holds up his hand & shakes his head & so I give it to Billy, who gladly accepts, then stuffs a handful in his mouth & chews. Then I demand a picture of Gregory & Billy before I forget, before the drugs do their thing, & they stand beside each other, Billy's arm wrapped around Gregory's neck, pulling Gregory closer, the hand of Billy's outstretched arm flipping the bird, & Gregory's white face is expressionless, except for the bright-red smile stretching from ear to ear, & Billy screws up his face, twisting his lips, standing about 6 inches shorter than Gregory, & I line up my cellphone till both Billy & Gregory fit on the screen & I press the OK button & a flash of light forces Gregory to squint, & the screen freezes the 2 of them in time, permanently.

Lemme see, Billy says.

I show him as Gregory looks over his shoulder, then whispers to me:

We should probably go.

Not now, I say.

I walk away, ignoring him outa spite for his stupid suggestion, because Billy's great & Gregory's being a total buzz-kill, & then things start moving & the party's only picking up, so I sit beside Jeremy again & he stands up & leaves, the fuckin asshole, & I flip him off as he disappears thru a doorway, closing the door behind him. Billy sits beside me & Gregory sits on the other side so I'm in the middle, & the walls are breathing now; it's unbelievable.

Things seem all disjointed & shit & everything's happening so fast, & Billy's saying stuff & I'm responding as Gregory is—where the fuck is he anyway?

I roll off the couch & land on my hands & knees & stare at the gray-carpeted floor, which is so close to my face, & spinning & rising & falling & it's like the ocean & I'm riding the waves & it's great, so fuckin great, &, O yea, where the fuck's Gregory? I forgot all about him. I stand up & Billy's still on the couch laughing like Tickle Me Elmo, which is hysterical in itself. I search for Gregory & stumble thru the open door & enter a room, the walls of which are covered with various posters, & across from me is a bunk bed & some guy's lying on the top bunk reading a magazine, & it feels as if a corkscrew's being shoved in my brain, twisting & twisting, & everything looks all distorted & screwed up, as though I'm trapped inside a kaleidoscope. I laugh & drool dribbles out the corner of my mouth & suddenly Gregory's standing next to me.

We should probably go, he says again.

I walk away & back into the common room & sit next to Billy again & he's still laughing & I join in on the laughter because everything's hysterical, & then more stuff happens, & then more, & then more, & ...

... straddling Billy, I lift the pipe in the air & bash him a few more times & blood splatters in my face & I'm smiling, just loving it, till something grabs me from behind & pulls me away, dragging me as Billy's beaten body is convulsing in the parking lot, & ...

... I look left & am frightened to see that the Joker's driving the car I'm in & my heart's trying to break outa my chest & I can feel sweat streaming down my face & I take a drag off my cigarette & …

… I look left & am frightened to see that the Joker's driving the car I'm in & my heart's trying to break outa my chest & I can feel sweat streaming down my face & I take a drag off my—where's my cigarette gone?—& …

… I look left & am frightened to see that the Joker's driving the car I'm in & my heart's trying to break outa my chest & I can feel sweat streaming down my face & I take a drag off my cigarette & …

… I look left & am frightened to see that the Joker's …

You OK? the Joker says.

The stars in the sky spin circles as I watch intently, fascinated, lying on the … the—where am I? a field?—& …

… I look left & am frightened to see that the Joker's driving the car I'm in & my heart's trying to break outa my chest & I can feel sweat streaming down my face & I take a drag off my cigarette, then exhale a cloud of smoke, which drifts out the open window. I twist the volume nob clockwise & "Born to Lose" by Johnny Thunders & the Heartbreakers is playing, already halfway into the song, & I sing along, half-mumbling.

You OK? says Gregory.

What happened?

You beat the shit outa Billy—don't you remember?—& we had to book it.

But why?

When he doesn't respond, I shrug away any last worry I might have about Billy & reach out in front of me & twist the volume nob even farther clockwise, cranking the music so loud I can feel my ear drums crying out in pain. Then I look left &—*WHAT THE FUCK!*—the Joker's driving the car I'm in & my heart begins beating faster & faster, trying to break outa my chest while sweat's streaming down my face, & I take a drag off my cigarette &....

The Haunted Bathroom

A short story....

"... roaring fiercely, as if a strip of fabric is torn in half, each stitch pulled apart, the sound magnified as if my ass is an amplifier, my butt cheeks fluttering ..."

"WHAT ARE YOU DOING?"

What was that? Sitting on a toilet, my dirty blue jeans wrapped around my ankles, I look left, then right. I ease myself off the toilet bowl, onto the grimy floor, landing on my knees. Bending over as close to the sticky slimy floor as possible, my face almost touching it, I look under the walls to my left and right, looking for feet, and I see none.

"What are you doing?" I hear it again.

"Who's there?" I say uneasily.

In response, a high-pitched chuckle ... a child laughing.

I stand up. Then I pull up my pants and fasten my belt tightly. I take a deep breath, not too thrilled about leaving the safety of my stall, before I open the door slowly. Then I hear the ghostly laughter again as I creep through the opening. *Drip, drop!* The faucet is leaking and in the silence that is all I can hear. That ... and the child laughing. I step forward.

"Where are you going?"

The door behind me slams shut, and I quickly glance over my shoulder, investigating the *thump!*

I have to get out of here.

I start toward the bathroom door, and the dripping stops. I continue to tiptoe toward the door, without missing a beat.

The lights flicker off and on.

I stop in my tracks. A breeze brushes by me, and so I look around, checking for open windows, of which there are none. It is then when I charge out the bathroom door, and—

I enter the bathroom. What the fuck! I try again, repeating myself, bolting out the bathroom door, and—

I enter the bathroom. What is going on? I appear to be trapped. Come to think of it, I cannot for the life of me remember how I ended up in here. I pace back and forth, while my hand caresses my chin, rubbing the stubble with my pointer finger. It feels like sandpaper. What was I doing before now? I try really hard to remember, to think back.

I was in a store.

No.

Yes, a store, surrounded by racks of various bottles. A liquor store? Yes, that has to be it. And I was nervous as I walked into the store. Why was I nervous?

Think!

I was sick too. Dope sick, I think. Immersed in cold sweats. Ice-cold sweat dripping down my face, my neck, my back, I entered the store and walked to the front. That is it. I whipped a gun out of my pants and held it at the cashier. He must have shot me or something.

No.

I was running from someone. The police? Yes. They were shooting at me as I hooked left into a narrow alley. I ran down the alley, brick walls on both sides, and stopped when I discovered that the alley had led me to a dead end.

My only exit, the way I had come in, blocked off, I searched eagerly for an alternate route. I climbed on top of the dumpster, hoping to vault over the wall, when company reared its ugly face.

There was one cop.

No.

Two cops! And they were holding guns, pointing them at me. What happened then?

Think!

As I climbed off the dumpster I was scared. I did not know what my best course of action would be. So I retrieved my gun and mimicked the cops, holding the Glock stiffly in my hand, pointing it straight ahead, and—

BANG!!!

The bullet, if I remember correctly, rocketed through the air, piercing my …

… heart?

And now I am here, in a public bathroom of some sort, with no escape. Am I dead? Is this hell? It cannot—

"What are you doing?"

Then I stop. Something unsettling has been brewing in my stomach. I grab my stomach, bend over, and release a short but agonizing moan. When a blast tears out of my ass, roaring fiercely, as if a strip of fabric is torn in half, each stitch pulled apart, the sound magnified as if my ass is an amplifier, my butt cheeks fluttering, slapping together, vibrating loudly, the pain settles slightly, and then the buzzing stops … an air bubble pops … a pig squeals as a moist discharge oozes out, settling in my pants.

I have shat myself.

I then remember why I was in here in the first place—I need to take a shit—as a rotten smell, like festering roadkill, slowly fills the room, lingering in the once pure air.

"Ew, gross!" says the eerie voice.

"Shut up!" I snap.

The unsettling painful pressure has returned to my stomach. I grip my protruding beer gut and storm back into the stall, drop my pants and sit heavily, my bear ass slapping the cold horseshoe-shaped seat. I push ...

... "ugh," comes out of my mouth.

I moan forcefully ...

... *"ha, ha, ha"* ...

... the high-pitched chuckle again ...

... *"ha, ha, ha"* ...

... *Plop!* ...

... one brick has fallen in the murky water ...

... *Plop!* ...

... a second brick ...

... *Plop!* ...

... one final brick ...

... a toilet flushes....

A toilet has flushed! That means ...

... I am not alone!

"Hello?" I say.

"Who's there?" asks my fellow patron, sounding startled.

I reach for toilet paper, but my hand hits an empty dispenser. No toilet paper. I do not care.

After I have pulled up my pants, fastened my belt, left the small cubicle, I am knocking on the neighboring stall.

Then the door slams open; a man, short but husky, long hair tied in a ponytail behind his head, a Metallica shirt hung loosely around his upper body, biceps bulging, baggy pants fastened to his waist with a studded belt, and big black engineer boots gripping the floor, is standing in front of me, practically stunned, awestruck eyes boring deep into my own, seeing through me, as if I am not really here.

And to him I am not, because he has just walked through me, now standing behind me.

I turn around and focus my attention on the strange man looking left, then right, then left, then right. It is like he has heard something that he just cannot make sense of, like the puzzle is missing a piece ...

... and I am the missing piece....

No, impossible.

Slowly and audibly: "Hello?" I say.

He turns and says, "Who said that?"

"What are you looking at, mister?" says the mysterious youthful voice.

"Hello?" I repeat, unsure as to who I am addressing—the ghost or the man?

"Who's there?" says the man in front of me, who, startled, faces the door and walks toward it, reaches for the handle as I watch. Twists the knob and flings the door open, then makes a quick exit, sprinting ...

... entering the bathroom.

Just like me he is trapped. But the fool tries again and enters the same way he went out.

I laugh at his third escape attempt, finding the insanity to be slightly amusing, that he so desperately wants to get out—even though we are in the same mess—and he tries again, failing for the fourth time.

"What are you doing?"

My eyes are trained on him, drifting left and right and left and right, as he paces back and forth, back and forth, then enters a stall, where my vision ends. I enter an adjacent stall and sit down on the toilet, the only place to sit, and think deeply. This is really starting to piss me ...

... *Plop!* ...

... off ...

... *Plop!* ...

An awful stench rises, and I shout, "How about a courtesy flush?"

Then when a familiar pain returns to my stomach, as if my bowels are squeezed in a vice, the merciless grip tightening, an unbearable pressure, a mole bobbing for air, I start to understand the strangeness that manifests in this eerie outlandish bathroom, a strangeness unlike any I have seen before—and my whole life has been a string of oddities, strange happenings, starting with when I was born, ass first, with a plastic spoon in my mouth—but this, however; this odd surreal reality I have entered unknowingly and unwillingly; this twisted queer center with no way out, no escape; this, this, *this:*

This is hell.

And I will forever have to shit.

And my only company is the ghost voice and a man that cannot see me.

And I have figured out exactly why this is:

The ghost voice must be of a child who has died before me. How long before me? I do not know.

And the man who I will forever haunt has died sometime after me.

And the man will haunt another being that I will not be able to see nor hear.

Just like how something, or someone, is haunting the child that has died before me.

And I will rot in this godforsaken void forever and ever and ever and ever and ever ...

... to be continued ...

... and ever and ever and ever and ever....

The Backseat Feud

A short story….

*"… leading into a manic guitar riff and a heavy drumbeat that sounds like a fast clock [**ticktockticktock**] plugged into murderous subwoofers …"*

SITTING IN A MEETING FOR recovery from alcoholism, I relax my head on Samantha's soft shoulder. She does not usually attend these meetings, but out of respect for me she agreed to go. Sporting a pair of red high-top Converse; tight black stretch jeans forced inside her Converse; a silver-pyramid-studded black-vegan-leather belt securely fastened to her waist, entwined through her belt loops, upholding her pants; a navy-green sleeveless collared shirt, POGO spray-painted in black across the center, buttoned up—four buttons vertically positioned from the collar down, assembling a V when unbuttoned—and covering her shirt is a red-plaid flannel letting off an aroma I just can't get enough of, so infinitely calming and remarkably comforting that I disperse into a euphoric nothing, my head perched on her shoulder, my eyes half-closed, my mind and body cascading into a peaceful undisturbed slumber ["Eric, wake-up," she whispers / "What?" / "The meeting's over"], Samantha shoves me awake. I ease my eyes open, observing the entire room—the alcoholics—scatter to their feet. I do the same, but first, I reach down next to my right foot, where my abandoned half-cup of coffee waits to be devoured, which is what I do: I dump the contents down my throat. Everyone's hands fuse together, forming an imperfect circle ["God," an old man says / **"God,"** everyone repeats. **"Grant me the serenity to accept the things I cannot change, the courage to change the things I can, and the wisdom to know the difference. Please"**]. Before severing the circle, all our hands flutter spasmodically. I forgot to mention Samantha's beautiful matching long brown hair—which also gives off that unique euphoric fragrance—and big brown eyes. ***Goddammit,*** *I love her*.

It's me, Samantha, and Samantha's best friend, Loren [who says, "You can't smoke weed in her car," into her phone matter-of-factly / "…" / "Eric gets piss tested" / "…" / "I know what we always do" / "…" / "Can't you wait thirty minutes?"]. We walk to Samantha's car. Displaying a light-blue denim long-sleeve jacket layered with various band patches and studs, Loren turns to Samantha [and says, "James is in a bad mood. He says he's going to smoke in the car no matter what anybody says" / "Tell him he can smoke before the drive or when we get there," Samantha says. "He'll manage" / "I did" / "Fuck it," I offer. "It's not a big deal if he smokes" / "Okay, I'll send him a text"]. We approach Samantha's car ["Loren," Samantha says, "I'll see you tonight" / "Bye," Loren replies, as she ambles away], only Samantha and I, Loren waving goodbye as she goes ["Bye," Samantha sings]. Samantha and I enter her car.

In the car, the music demolishing our ear drums, I rotate the volume nob counterclockwise, silencing the disquiet ["You know," I say, "maybe it's not such a great idea if James smokes. I really shouldn't be around weed" / "I'll text Loren to let her know" / "Thanks"]. Then I twist the volume nob clockwise, excessively cranking the noise, cigarette smoke coolly wafting out the open windows, Samantha to my left, right hand on the wheel, controlling the car, puffing on her cigarette [... **inhale** ... **exhale** ...], nodding her head up and down in sync with the loud fast beat, both of us shouting:

"I can't stand the peace and quiet.
All I want is a-a runnin' riot.
I can't stand the peace and quiet.
All I want is a-a runnin' ... **RIOT**."

We pull up to James's house, park on the side of the road. Standing on the sidewalk, Loren waits. She opens up the back door [and says, "Hey" / "Hey," Samantha and I both say], then enters ["Where's James?" Samantha asks / "Just getting out of the shower. He'll be out in a minute"]. "AU" by Cock Sparrer ends and "Riot Squad" by Cock Sparrer begins: a police siren bellows from the speakers, leading into a manic guitar riff and a heavy drum beat that sounds like a fast clock [**ticktockticktock**] plugged into murderous subwoofers and a vibrating trash can mashed together and put into a blender—the blender being the guitar—and the end result crashes and smashes and bashes and fumbles and tumbles out of the speakers, drowning out all thoughts ["**When we were at school I thought we had it sussed; fighting the law with the rest of us; smoking, drinking, acting cool; they started treating him like a fool!**" the stereo hollers, via the speakers], bouncing from wall to wall to wall, shaking the car, stirring us up all crazy-like.

We sit in the parked car, bobbing our heads in time to Cock Sparrer, like rhythmic bobble-head dolls, when James enters, his chicken-hawk charged up and ready to go. Samantha to my left, Loren behind me, and James behind Samantha, we drive away—nothing but **smoooooth** sailing—soon bearing onto I-95 toward Boston.

Five minutes pass and James pulls a one-hitter from his pocket. I glance at him explosively ["If you light that thing," I warn authoritatively, "I'll throw it out the window"]. He puts his puny one-hitter away. Not another word is spoken as we cruise ahead. Bluffing I was not when I said I would toss his one-hitter out the window. I can't afford a dirty urine analysis. An awkward dissatisfying humdrum silence defiles the bitter air in which we breathe. *Somebody, do something!*

Ten minutes later I open my window, light a cigarette ["**I don't smoke cigarettes!**" James wines. "**If he can smoke cigarettes, why can't I smoke weed?!**" / "This is my car," Samantha explains, "and cigarettes are allowed"]. Finally, the uncomfortable wretched silence escapes the car, replaced with cigarette smoke and injustice ["**That's not fair!**" James continues. "**He shouldn't be allowed to smoke cigarettes! If I can't smoke weed he can't smoke cigarettes!**"]. I clench my ready fists but don't desire an uproar, puffing on my cigarette anxiously with shorter intervals between each puff ["**That's not fair! You can't smoke cigarettes, Eric! Not if I can't smoke weed!**"]. *Do the right thing, Eric,* I keep telling myself, because if I do the right thing ["**That's not fair!**"] I'll get the right results, *but* ["**I don't smoke—**" / "**SHUT THE FUCK UP!!!**" I snap] *fuck the right thing* ["**Or I'm coming back there!**" / "Come back here!" James challenges]. In one swift fluid out-of-control act of violence, I turn around and my forceful fist jet-rockets into James's nose, crushing my cigarette, and blood splatters everywhere, as if he got shot in the face with a red paintball—in the direct center of his face. I wind up my arm, almost like I'm winding up an invisible bow-and-arrow—as James attempts to shield himself with his stringy arms and legs, curling up into a ball (or more like the fetal position), but in his drunken inadequate state, is unsuccessful at that—abruptly releasing the elastic, and jam my knuckles into his breakable jaw. I punch him yet **again** and **againagainagainagainagainagainagain**, unleashing all the aggression I have built up in the previous couple of months (James is in the wrong place at the wrong time, I can promise you that). Satisfied, I turn back around to face the fleeting road. The rotten silence returns. *What was I thinking?* ... and ... and ... the uncomfortable silence grows more and more and more unbearably misanthropic ... and [**whack!**] James sucker-punches me in the side of my pretty face—*here we go again*—knocking me sideways; my hard head almost crashes into the window. *Big mistake*. I turn around and go at him again—*fun, fun, fun*—this time with more destructive force. I smack him around violently, hitting him in the side of his deformed face, his jaw, and his head **againagain** ["Stop hitting my boyfriend!" Loren screams, panicking] **againagain** ["**Stop!**"] **againagain**. Loren tries to pull me off of him, but with my adrenalin rushing through my empty veins, like electricity zipping through ruthless wires, I'm an unstoppable force, beating her boyfriend to a pulp **againagainagain**, and ... one more time for good luck: I slap him with the inside of my hand, right across his face, leaving a bright red imprint. James has learned his lesson. He knows if he tries anything again, **I am ready**; I do not bluff. Samantha accelerates down I-95 toward Boston ["Eric," she says, seemingly pissed, "both times you went back there you knocked the car into neutral," but seemingly turned on by what just happened too / "Turn the car around!" James demands. "I wanna go home" / "C'mon," Samantha says. "Shit happens. That was Punk rock" / "You got blood on my jacket," Loren complains / "Shit happens"]. I, at this point in time, *Let go, let God*, as they say: I do not say a word, allowing the perturbed madness to play itself out ["Turn the car around," James sobs / "That was Punk rock. Eric, say you're sorry. Both of you, shake hands and make up. C'mon, you guys. MDC. Subhumans. Shake hands and make up" / "I wanna go home," James cries out]. Then, sadly, she merges off I-95, takes two right turns, and becomes a part of I-95 toward Beverly. *Mess with the best, end up like the rest: beaten and bloody.*

We park at James's house, drop off James and Loren, drive away, and then we are back on I-95 toward Boston ["I feel like such an idiot," I confess / "Why?" / "I lost it back there" / "So what? It was Punk rock. What's a show without the pre-show fight?"]. *She doesn't seem to understand* ["I **had** complete control, but he crossed the line, and someone **had** to do something or he wouldn't shut up" / "It's not a big deal," Samantha shrugs and sort of laughs / *I just wish I didn't have to be that someone*, I don't mention, but instead: "I guess it's kind of funny," I lie, and force a smile].

We park our car somewhere in Central Square, Cambridge, ready for the show, drinking Monsters ["They're not gonna let us in the show with these Monsters, you know?" I mention]. We open the doors and step outside ["I know," Samantha says. "What should we do?" / "We could stash them, I guess. Like in the old days. When we used to hide our bottles in the bushes somewhere near the show" / "Let's just leave 'em in the car" / "That could work too, but we'll have to come back to the car if we want more" / "They'll most likely serve Red Bulls at the bar" / "Yea," I agree, "that's true. I hope they serve Monsters"].

We stroll four to five blocks to the show, excited, where we join the end of a long line sticking out the front door, concocting a ninety-degree angle, stretching along the brick wall side of the venue. We wait (the doors, according to BostonPunk.org, were supposed to open at eight p.m., and it is—I check my cell phone—eight-o'four p.m.) and wait and—

Mutual friends of ours, all dressed similar, big black boots and jeans and studded black leather biker jackets and outrageous hairstyles—Jay, a shaved head; Katie, an orange Chelsea-hawk; Chris, half-red half-black liberty spikes—approach us, say hi, and we all walk off toward Wendy's, where **they** plan to eat. (Samantha and I have already eaten.) Chris, my only friend who has **always** been there for me, puts his arm around my neck, taking me from the crowd [and asks, "Wanna go get drunk?"]—typical Chris ["No," I reply. "I don't drink anymore" / "Why not?" he asks, genuinely concerned / "I can't be with Samantha if I continue to drink" / "I'm sorry to hear that" / "Not a problem. I've tried to quit many times in this past year, but nothing has worked. Not until Samantha came back into my life, at least"]. Chris offers me a confused look ["Well," he says, "then I'm glad for you. If it makes you happy," he adds, seeming proud of me, "you have my blessing" / "Thanks," I say sarcastically. "That means a lot to me"]. Chris and I follow the crowd, five to ten feet behind, as Samantha shares the craziness from earlier today with our friends ["Blood," she concludes, "was everywhere" / "That sounds like Eric," I hear a friend say]. *That sounds like **me**?* I ponder that remark, unsure of what to think or how to re-act. That sounds more like Eric Rampage, not Eric Derelict, the new and improved Eric—the new and improved **me**, Eric McKenzie.

Everybody indulges at Wendy's, except for Samantha and myself. Then we all leave, heading back to the show. The line is long gone by the time we get back. I hurry to the door ["Eric," comes from behind me]. Upon turning around I eyeball—*not again*—James. He's back for more and I don't really want to give him more [*Fuck off*, I think about saying]. But my reputation might get challenged. So I stand ready [surprisingly: "Sorry," James mumbles]. James, the bigger man, apparently ["I'm sorry too," I utter warily]. *What got into him?* I wonder. We shake hands and make up. *The past is the past—**was** the past*—we agree.

I creep through the front door of the venue, pay the large bouncer the necessary evil—ten dollars—to enter, descend the narrow staircase, and then bump into Bob—literally bump into him, nearly knocking him over, spilling his beer ["Watch where you're going!" he hisses]. Bob looks frustrated, angry, wide-eyed and bloodshot ["Dude," I say, "I'm sorry"], a tad bit tipsy. The venue is dark; the only light comes from the stage. A thousand silhouettes stand and talk. A big smile erupts on Bob's face ["Wait a second ... Eric?" / "Yea, Bob, it's me, you drunken prick" / "How's it going?" / "Not bad. Not bad at all. How—" / "I," he interrupts me, "hear you don't drink no more" / "No, I don't" / "You don't do drugs either?" / "No, not anymore. I'm—" / "That," he cuts me off, "doesn't sound like you" / "No. No, it doesn't. I was abducted by aliens. I can't wait for the show to start. I've seen the Subhumans, like, a handful of times, but I've never seen MDC. I'm psyched" / "Me too"] and I walk away.

The first two bands play. They are all right, but I preserve my energy. Standing up, leaning back against a wall, Samantha to my left, my arm stretched around her neck, my hand gently clutching her shoulder, both of us facing forward, toward the stage, Samantha looks at me ["You wanna go for a walk?" she asks / "What for?" / "I need to get some tampons. Then take them to the car, 'cause I don't wanna get searched nor the security guard to find tampons on me; that would be embarrassing"]. *One more band ... then MDC, then the Subhumans. We have time* ["Yea, let's go," I say]. *But **why** does she need tampons **now**?*

We leave the show together, walk along Mass Ave., arrive at CVS, enter the store, then leave with what we came here for—a box of tampon concealed in a CVS plastic bag—and the adventure begins: *where's Samantha's car?* Walking all over the place, we search and search and search, finding no car nowhere. This reminds us of the good ol' drunken nights, the nights when we would lose the car every time we brought it out. Samantha and I joke and laugh about this memory ["It's kind of ironic that we can't find the car, but we're sober, don't you think?" she says].

Night Flight

A short story....

"... as if the plane were completely still and connected to a rod that riotously rocked the cabin ..."

YOU SIT ON THE OTHER side of airport security, pretending to read a novel by Jeff Strand, but really listening to the fat family of three sitting across from you talk loudly and incessantly about God knows what. You want them ... *need* them to shut up or you won't be able to focus. Usually you focus quite well with others around and talking, but the sight of the young girl getting out of the pilot's seat had sent unsettling thoughts racing through your mind, and now you're easily agitated, and those fat fucks sitting across the way won't shut the fuck up. You need to relax. Breathe in, breathe out. Focus on the book in your hand. Forget about the fat family. You'll only be in their company for close to another hour and a half. So relax. Take it easy. Breathe deeply. You can do it.

A guy dressed in white opens the door and beckons for you and the others in attendance to come with him to the plane. You're the first one to follow, the first one to give up your bag to be stored in the left wing, the first one to ascend the four steps leading to the plane, the first one through the door. You decide you'll sit up front, right behind where the copilot would sit, right behind where the old man behind you would sit, if only the girl pilot doesn't hold up her hand and count how many passengers will be flying with you. But she does; you watch her count five and realize there is room for everybody even if nobody sits in the copilot's seat.

She cranes her neck so as to look at the old man and says, "That seat's reserved for full flights only."

He sits down to your left and pouts.

You feel for this man. He was looking forward to sitting up front next to the pretty pilot. Really it has nothing to do with her beauty, although she is rather beautiful; he just wants to see the view through the pilot's perspective.

Which you know nothing about. Most times you fly from Rutland, VT, to Boston, MA—every time, actually—you spend the whole hour and however many minutes reading a book or writing a short story in your notebook.

But you've never flown at night before, and the whole cabin is dark, way too dark to read. You search for a light and see your own personal light overhead, pointed at you. You push up against the button beside the bulb, and your whole seat starts to glow. Good.

But when the girl turns on the engine the light flickers out.

Not good. Not good at all. Will the light go back on once the plane is in motion? Hopefully it does.

She swivels in her seat and faces you, and her smooth skin is free of blemishes. She is so young, as if she had come here straight from college, as if this flight tonight is her first flight ever. You have nothing against women flying planes. No, of course not. That would be bigotry, and you are not a bigot. But you are a little wary of her flying this particular plane. If you weren't a passenger, though, you'd have nothing against it. But you are, and you hope this is just a cruel joke. You contemplate asking her how many flights she has done, but decide after all to just suck it up and hope for the best.

She goes over with you and the others the standard operating procedures, like where to find your lifejacket and how to use it if your life's in jeopardy. She says nothing new, nothing you haven't heard before, though she leaves out whether she has any family, whether she has any reason to live. Maybe she doesn't. Maybe she has a death wish. You really ought to be thinking positive thoughts right now. Rather than focusing on the quiver in her voice, you should listen to what she has to say. It very well could save your life.

"... It's going to be a very bumpy ride," she says.

Okay, maybe you shouldn't have listened. But it's too late now, although you would have found that out eventually, when the plane takes flight, so why does it matter?

She turns back around and props her earmuff-sized headphones over her head.

You wonder where the usual pilot is. Probably on your first flight from Rutland to Boston, you heard him tell another passenger that he has a family, and knowing that surely settled your anxieties about flying on such a small plane, so small that they have no need for a copilot—but what if something happens to the pilot? It's quite unlikely that a passenger on a seven-passenger plane would be trained to take over.

The plane starts forward then, following the trail of bright red lights on the runway. It then turns to follow a path of blue lights. Then turns to follow a trail of orange lights. Then back to blue. This is strange. You don't remember it ever being this long before you took off. Usually the plane picks only one color and, while following the chosen color all the way to the end of the runway, speeds up so fast that soon after, the nose rises and points upward and the whole plane plows into the sky.

But now the plane just stops and sits idly.

She turns to face you again. "I can't take off for another fifteen minutes," she informs you and the others. "There is a much bigger plane coming down now, and I have to wait for it to land."

"Does this light not work?" you ask, anticipating another boring fifteen minutes and an even more boring flight.

"It's not safe to fly with it on at night," she says.

That's fucked up, you decide not to say.

You feel a pestering form of panic start to grow inside you. Don't worry. It won't be long before you're in Boston. Just take deep breaths. Easy does it. Whatever you do, don't panic. Don't overreact. Things will be fine. And if things are not fine, well, it's too late now.

It is a slow fifteen minutes which soon slips out of existence, and the plane starts to move again. Finally. The plane picks up speed and at a slight angle, lifts off the ground and goes airborne, entering the dark sky, as if a black hole were pulling you into its vacuum.

Then, instantly the plane whips left, right, up, down, up, down again, and you hold onto the back of the copilot's seat for support as the plane staggers violently through the sky while ascending at a forty-five-degree angle to the dark clouds above. Out the window you can see falling snow that seems like motionless white stars. The turbulence doesn't stop there, though. It keeps on pushing and pulling the plane in a tug-of-war where both sides are equally matched and getting madder and tugging harder as the plane penetrates the dark cloud. Everything goes dark for a moment, and while pushing through the cloud a jagged line of light strikes right in front of the plane. The whole cloud lights up, like a snapshot taken in a dark room, as the rod of lightning flies right past like a javelin headed straight to Earth. The snowflakes glow for a moment before the light fades and the "bumpy ride" knocks the plane down for what feels like a twenty-foot drop. Your stomach flips and then flops as the wind pushes the plane up and down again, and you can see the dim light through the front window, the plane surfacing above the clouds and flattening.

Then the turbulence eases away. You release your grip on the seat and ease your fingers over the back and set them in your lap. You look out the window and are mesmerized by the sight, as if you were hovering over a purple fluffy ocean. A dark purple. It seems you have entered Heaven, and your eyes widen as you wonder how close to the clouds you actually are. The plane, it appears, is grazing the top. Serenity seeps into your head, and all you can think about is the beautiful view. Who would have thought?

You've lost yourself in it.

You wonder if the others on the plane can see the same. Does it matter if they can see the same? Sure, it does. You brainstorm ways you might show this to others who haven't actually seen it. The whole sky is a dark shade of purple that seems to darken as it gets higher until it fades into black. It all looks godlike.

The plane soars forward and the view soon fades as the plane plows into another cloud.

Lightning flashes only once, and soon you're enveloped in darkness.

The plane careens this way and that, but it doesn't seem as frightening as the last bit of turbulence, because being in this total darkness gives off the feeling that you're only in a flight simulator, as if the plane were completely still and connected to a rod that riotously rocked the cabin.

But still, you hold onto the seat in front of you. Just relax. It will be okay. You'll see.

And then the plane bounces, like a car running over a rut in the road, before emerging out the other end of the cloud, and you have entered Hell. The dark Earth's surface is dotted with Christmas tree lights, and maneuvering around the many illuminated dots, thin rivers of fire flow, following the windy paths through the black horizon that only shows any color whatsoever where the lone lights glow. The rivers intersect in many places and proceed through until the flames flow in single file again and then wind their way past more lone lights.

Here the turbulence remains minimal, a few bumps here and there, but after what you've been through, it's only expected. You can relax now. The plane is slowly but surely going down, and maybe you can see the towers that make up Boston, the monuments of the city. Oh yes, you can see them, with lights rhythmically flashing on the rooftops. You've almost arrived. Safely.

You're so close you can see the runway now.

You feel the floor tremble slightly and know it's only the wheels being lowered. A smile holds your face hostage then, and a chuckle of relief seeps through your teeth.

You sneak a peek over the copilot's seat and out the front window, and before and under the plane is Boston. You watch the city as it comes closer and grows larger all the way until the darkness opens up for the runway which is coming closer and closer and—*thunk*.

You have arrived. The plane is soaring across the runway at high speeds but slowing down drastically until it stops completely. You crane your neck to check if the other passengers are as pleased as you. The old man is fast asleep and the three fatties each share the same look of forlorn on their faces, but the fifth passenger—a girl about your age, give or take—is absolutely stunning. Why hadn't you noticed her before?

You are staring into her eyes when the cabin door opens up, and she returns the stare with annoyance, her eyes angled inward, brows shaped like a V. You divert your gaze, feelings of rejection meandering in your mind. You need a distraction. Something that will make you forget about the bitch in back. So you *clap-clap-clap* your hands rapidly and loudly. But all alone. No one else joins in. You've been on other planes and know it's customary for the passengers to applaud the pilot for a successful flight. You stop clapping and rest your hands in your lap.

It's only you and the old man and the girl pilot left on the plane, you only now notice, everybody else having ditched through the open door. Maybe that's why no one clapped with you.

You look left and the old man is still fast asleep. You think about waking him. But you decide to do something much more daring, as waking him is not your responsibility. You tap the pilot on her shoulder. She remains unresponsive. You tap her twice more.

She turns and faces you and is smiling brightly. Clearly she must be pleased about the plane's successful landing too.

"Sir, we're waiting for you," comes from outside the door.

You ignore him, instead addressing the pilot:

"Thank you," you say.

Her smile widens.

"What did you say your name was?"

She says, "Sharon."

"Well, Sharon—"

"Sir!"

You whip your head around and hurl at him a fierce grin, one that clearly states, *Not now.*

The pilot is still looking at you when you refocus your attention on her.

"Again, thank you."

And then you do the unthinkable. You press your palm on the back of her head and pull her toward you and plant a sweet kiss on those sweet lips.

But she jerks back and her hand crashes into your face.

You get off the plane with your head hung down. Why did you do that? What could you have been thinking?

Stink-Box

A short story....

"... cruising in the left lane on Rt. 9, passing cars on my right, listening to Anti-Nowhere League, staring out the open window and enjoying the wind on my face ..."

MONDAY MORNING AT EIGHT I go to work at Panera Bread. I walk past the cashiers and into the back to clock in. As I punch my password in the computer I hear:

"What happened to your eye?"

I divert my gaze to the direction of the voice, and it's my manager.

Since I haven't looked in the mirror this morning I say: "What do you mean?"

"Your eye is black."

I think about that. Why is my eye black?

"Oh yea." I finally remember....

IT HAD ALL STARTED WHEN *he was younger and he would go out drinking with his mates, before he was known as Derek Defect; he would put on his headphones and zone out, until one day Fat Freddy told him it was rude to hang out with people and then pretend they didn't exist, disappearing into his own little private world. He liked drinking and he liked noise, so he had brilliantly invested in a boom-box. He could keep his tunes* and *associate with people, his so-called friends. He began buying cheap boom-boxes at*

CVS for twenty to forty bucks, but they would always break. He probably went through one every couple of months. At one point he had a small tape player, which had a speaker on it, to play music out loud with (that tape player was his favorite music player he'd ever owned, small yet loud, convenient), but he left it at the bank. Then he bought another boom-box at CVS for thirty bucks, which stopped playing one day after he had spilt beer all over it. What a shame that had been! So he bought another similar boom-box, which he accidentally threw out the window of a pickup truck on the highway.

One night in Harvard Square, Derek hitched a ride home with Katie, from Bob Nonsense, who hated Derek because Derek, but not him, had fucked Katie. Bob was jealous.

Bob, who was expected to drive, was wasted, just like the rest of them, and Katie was too worried to ride in a car with Bob driving. So Derek told her he would come along himself and keep her safe, as if he were her safety blanket, giving her the illusion of safety, and she talked Bob into taking Derek home too, which was thirty to forty-five minutes out of Bob's way. Bob didn't want to drive Derek home, but since Bob had a hopeless crush on Katie he clearly said yes.

Katie, Bob, and Derek took the train from Harvard Square to Alewife, where Bob had parked his pickup truck. Bob would drive, Derek would ride in the passenger seat, Katie on his lap, and his boom-box was carefully placed in the bed of Bob's truck. After they dropped off Katie in Concord, MA, Bob and Derek would drive south to Newton, MA, where Derek lived with his parents and sister. On the way to Derek's parents' place, driving down Rt. 2, the highway that had taken them to Katie's, Derek wanted to play his own CD, which was in his boom-box, but forgot he had stored it safely in the back. When he realized his boom-box was in the back, a brilliant, if not belligerent, idea was born: Derek would climb out of the truck and into the bed heroically, rescue his CD, and reenter the fleeting truck in no time.

And that was exactly what he did, although he unfortunately dropped his boom-box and watched it bounce down the side of the highway. Derek watched regretfully as the boom-box rolled away, pieces breaking off as it pounded the pavement, fragments flying every which way, like a ball of yarn rolling and unraveling as it summersaults across the carpet.

NOW IN CHRIS'S RED PICKUP truck, Chris behind the wheel, I was riding effortlessly to the Natick Mall, cruising in the left lane on Rt. 9, passing cars on my right, listening to Anti-Nowhere League, staring out the open window and enjoying the wind on my face, like a dog. I wanted to buy a big red boom-box I had discovered two weeks ago in Sears in the Natick Mall. I couldn't wait. I wanted it, and I wanted it now. The boom-box, if I remembered correctly, was massive, like something a construction worker might use. I hoped it was still there. When I'd first found the boom-box I had wanted to steal it, but Fat Freddy, who'd driven me to the mall, was too much of a pussy to bring his car around and wait so I could make a quick exit.

"SO FUCKING WHAT?!" screamed from the speakers, and I turned the volume nob clockwise, upping the ante, so

to speak, because “So What?” was my favorite Anti-Nowhere League song.

Chris was bobbing his head like a bobble-head doll, eyes fixed on the road, and I joined in, bobbing my head in sync with the reckless rhythm, and we both began:

“Well,” screamed the song and so did we, *“I’ve been to hasting, and I’ve been to Brighton! I’ve been to Eastbourne too! So what?! So what?! … I’ve been here, and I’ve been there, and I’ve been every fucking where! So what?! So what?! So what, so what, you boring little cunt?! …”*

Chris and I drifted into the dark parking garage, drove to the top level, the unbearably bright spring sun beating down heavily, and parked in a designated spot marked with white paint. I was extremely excited to buy the boom-box. All my hours working at Panera Bread had, apparently, paid off.

We exited the truck and then entered the Natick Mall, strolling side by side, and then Sears, one-hundred-fifty bucks in my back pocket. I searched the huge store, as if on a mission from God, bouncing from aisle to aisle trying hard to remember where I’d found the boom-box two weeks ago, with Chris following suit.

Finally, I spotted the boom-box, which cost one-hundred dollars, ninety-nine cents, and after carrying the big rectangular box, the boom-box stored firmly inside, to the front, I paid the cashier, who passed back a penny, at the checkout counter.

“Keep the change,” I said.

“Thanks,” the cashier replied.

Chris and I ambled away, exiting the store and entering the mall. We soon settled in the food court sitting across from each other, the boom-box still in its box resting peacefully on the floor undisturbed next to my right foot. I'd bought pork ribs from the Chinese food restaurant, and he'd bought two slices of pizza, one cheese and one pepperoni.

Also, we'd both bought Cokes, of which we were taking sips as we ate.

"I think I'll call it my 'stink-box'," I said.

"That's cool," Chris said. "I'll be right back."

"Where you going?"

"The bathroom," he said, and stood.

Thinking long and hard as he walked away, I gave birth to another one of my brilliant ideas. I stood, turned, and marched straight to the bathroom, holding the boom-box in my left hand, the remaining pork ribs in my right, grinning mischievously, like I was about to do something stupid—and I was—Chris out of my line of sight.

Then I entered the bathroom silently, still carrying the remaining pork ribs, and set the "stink-box" down. Still grinning, I tiptoed toward Chris, who was standing at a urinal, feet shoulder length apart, back facing me. When I approached him I pushed the pork ribs in his face forcefully, pushing him backwards as piss dribbled down his leg.

"You fucking asshole!" he shouted as I just stood there laughing.

When he went to the sink to wash himself off, I turned my back, obviously not thinking clearly, because I had to take a piss, my bladder full, on the verge of exploding. I approached the urinal, unzipped my pants, pulled out my—

Something smacked me in the side of my face, and I screamed: "Cunt!"

Holding my throbbing right eye, I turned around and saw Chris standing behind him, gripping a CAUTION: WET FLOOR sign in both hands, bent over, laughing hysterically.

I was pissed. But it was like they say: *Payback's a bitch*. So I resumed, relieving myself in the urinal, a stream of yellow liquid arching through the air, splashing on the urinal cake. I contemplated picking up the piss-soaked cake and force-feeding it into Chris's mouth, but then thought better of it, because that would involve me having to touch the heinous cake too. My body trembled slightly at the sick thought.

Together we left the bathroom and then the mall and went to Newton, MA, where I bought an eighteen-pack of PBR and Chris bought a pint of Jäger. We hit the streets, testing my spanking-new "stink-box," which hung from Chris's right hand, for the first time ever, the truck parked at my parents' place, the beer and Jäger bouncing in my backpack, which was strapped loosely to my back. We crossed the street, the stereo blasting, and entered a wide-open park. Listening to Abrasive Wheels, we strolled through the empty park. We approached a street and turned right, Store 24 coming into view as we walked. Silence sat comfortably in the air, like an unspoken agreement, as we listened to the music.

Next to Store 24, we entered a Dunkin Donuts, where we asked for two cups of water, one each.

"Just a cup of water," Chris said.

"Is that all?" the cashier asked as she fetched one—

"Make that two," I said, the cashier fetching two cardboard cups, which she then filled with water and passed to both of us.

Chris and I took turns using the bathroom, emptying and filling up the cups with booze, me first, then him, me passing the backpack to him as we crossed paths outside the bathroom. Now satisfied, we left Dunkin Donuts.

Drinking—me, beer; Chris, Jäger—we strolled along more streets, the light eventually changing to dark. We crossed through a different field, the boom-box still blasting. At the far end of the field a loud woman's voice, coming from above, caught our attentions.

"Shut that shit off!"

Where the voice was coming from, we didn't know.

"Fuck off!" Chris said, looking up. I was looking up too.

"It's the middle of the night!"

"It's only ten-o'clock, you cunt," I said to the sky.

"I have work in the morning!"

"Shut up!"

"Then go to sleep!" Chris shouted.

"I'm going to bring down my shotgun!"

"Bring it," I said challengingly.

"Yea, bring it," Chris repeated.

Then we started throwing rocks aimlessly in the direction of the voice.

A satisfying silence.

Chris and I walked away, clearly up to no good, with trouble lurking around the corner.

A few streets later I had a funny thought, and now Chris needed to sit down, his world spinning out of control as he pressed POWER on the "stink-box," then sat on a bench on the side of the street; the full moon bright, my moonlit shadow looming over him, cars zipping by, muffled voices in the distance, trees waving in the wind. Then he tipped his Dunkin Donuts cup to his lips.

"You okay?" I asked.

"I just need to sit," he said. "You hit me really fucking hard."

Being the bastard that I was, I had hit him in the head, although rather lightly, but now he felt faint.

I said: "You sure you're not just drunk?"

"Positive."

"I only tapped you," I said, denying his claims.

"Well, your fists are fucking hard, then."

"Maybe."

After a moment he stood up and said: "I'm ready to go."

"You sure?" I asked.

"Yea, I'm ready."

"Ok, then let's—"

His elbow flew into my lip, splitting it in the center.

"Fuck!" I yelped, taken aback by the jolting unexpected blow to my jaw, blood spilling out, dripping down my chin.

"Now I'm ready to go," he said humorously, with a slight smile on his face, as I dabbed my own shirt on my bloody bruised lip.

Then he pressed POWER, followed by PLAY, allowing the music to commence. Now with Abrasive Wheels playing, he and I walked drunkenly toward the latter park we'd crossed, where we'd heard the heated woman's voice. We reached the park, and—

"Shut that shit off!" the same woman's voice fell from the sky.

Chris smiled anarchically.

"I said, shut that shit off!"

"Cunt!" I said.

Back and forth Chris and I traded rude remarks with the irate woman, who finally said:

"That's it, I'm calling the cops!"

"Fuck you," I said. "Bitch," Chris said.

"They'll be here any minute now!"

A moment later a light rotating from blue to red headed in our direction.

The cop car cruised toward us silently, then stopped. The front door opened with ease, and a boot smacked the pavement. Then a second boot. A small but muscular man, fully clad in cop clothing, came into view. His nametag read: OFFICER WELLS, but neither of us could read the small print.

"Derek, you again," Wells said.

"Yea, it's me," I said defiantly.

"Can you turn the music off?"

Chris turned a big black nob on top of the boom-box, the volume nob, counterclockwise, muting the music.

Wells said, "I need to see some ID."

"Why? Don't you remember me from four days ago?" I said, with a drunken smirk, and removed my black wallet from my back pocket, slid my ID out of its designated spot, and passed it to the police officer, with Chris doing the same.

"I remember you," Wells snapped. "I clocked out not even an hour after I dealt with you then," he snarled, "and it hasn't even been an hour since I clocked in tonight. The last two hours of work I had to deal with you. And both times you were bleeding." He grabbed both of our IDs.

"Wait right here!" Then entered his car, where he typed up both of our information on his computer.

Chris and I waited.

FOUR DAYS EARLIER FAT FREDDY, *Katie, and Derek went to a daytime show at the ICC Church together, although neither Katie nor Derek could get in because they didn't have enough money—ten dollars. So Derek and Katie went around back, where they spotted a door, a window on each side. Derek hatched another one of his brilliant plans: he would slam the door open with his shoulder, just charge into it using brute force. So that was what he did: he dashed into the door, but, unfortunately, he missed the door by a couple of inches, and his shoulder smashed through the glass window on the right side, the glass shattering and slashing open his shoulder—he was wearing a sleeveless shirt. Now that the window had been broken, he reached through the hole and unhitched the door.*

Then Freddy, Katie, and Derek fled from the church a little bit later because Derek and Katie found a fancy PA system in the basement. Freddy was already outside when Derek and Katie flew past. A bouncer chased them out of the church after discovering them down there trying to take the PA.

Later that night, after a full day of binge drinking—a typical Tuesday—Freddy, Katie, and Derek took the train to Newton, MA, just in time before the trains stopped running. Freddy had parked his car at Derek's parents' place and had to get back to his girlfriend, and Katie was going to crash with Derek.

Next to the Newton Highlands station, where the subway had brought the three of them, was a liquor store, a.k.a. a packy. Freddy had a long drive ahead of him, during which drinking would pass the time, and neither Derek's nor Katie's night had ended. So in the parking lot outside the packy Katie lit a cigarette as Derek and Freddy, blood dripping down Derek's bare arm, went into the store, through the electric sliding door, and as they strolled in freely, a synthesized ding let the clerk know they'd come in. Derek and Freddy, without wasting any time, went straight to the back, to the fridge, because the store would close in several minutes. Derek dislodged the glass door, the suction set free, and was ambushed by an uncomfortably cold breeze which brushed past his bare face, a gray mist floating frivolously from his mouth. Then he fingered four forty-ounces as Freddy fingered two. They took the drinks from the fridge and carried them to the front, where the Indian—or Arabic—clerk pulled out a baseball bat that had been hidden behind the desk and babbled a lot of broken English that neither of them could understand. Freddy and the clerk were caught in a screaming match, neither of them speaking coherently, as Freddy's words were slurred and the clerk—

The fuck was he saying?

Derek said Fuck it *silently and stole his four forty-ounces, quickly ditching the scene, while the distracted Packy was spewing nonsense at Freddy.*

Outside the store a cop—Officer Wells—was waiting for Derek and told Derek to wait right there, before Wells went into the store himself, and side by side he and Freddy came out. The cop ordered Freddy and Katie to leave New-

ton, NOW, and a bloody Derek was ordered to go home and stay there. But they all had to go to Derek's parents' place because Freddy's car had been parked there. Wells said that was fine, but if he saw any of them out again, off to jail they would go. Wells was letting them off with a warning, as they hadn't done anything wrong; they'd only wanted beer.

PRESENTLY WELLS PASSED ME AND Chris our IDs back and pointing accusingly at me said:

"Derek, if I see you out here again tonight I'll arrest you." Then, turning to look at Chris, added: "And Chris, keep your friend out of trouble, will you?"

The cop left, and Chris and I started to stagger to my parents' place, stopping at Store 24 on our way. He went inside the store to buy a bag of potato chips as I waited for him outside, with the boom-box still blaring, of course. Then out of nowhere I met a short heavyset boy with a Mohawk hung down.

"Nice Mohawk," I said.

"Thanks," the boy said, holding out his hand. "I'm Samuel."

"Derek Defect."

We shook hands.

"I've heard of you," he said.

"Everybody's heard—"

Chris left the store and said: "What's up?" gaining my attention.

Chris looked at Samuel, who was holding out his hand, waiting to shake, and he completely ignored Samuel's gesture, but instead said:

"We should probably go. The cop said—"

"Fuck the police," I hissed, and pulled a beer from my backpack, then sat on the curb. Samuel sat down next to me.

"Want a beer?" I asked him.

"No thanks," he said timidly, my can of PBR perched in between us, Chris pacing nervously, bobbing his head to the beat, singing along silently, the three of us listening to the Dead Boys now. I lifted my beer bravely, tipped it to my lips, and poured it in, then set it down when a police cruiser pulled into the parking lot, the blinking red-and-blue lights turned off. Out of the cruiser stepped—*what luck?*—Officer Wells, looking more pissed than ever.

He said: "Well, well, boys. What a surprise."

Chris glanced at me and murmured: "I told you."

The two cops, Wells and company, went over the standard procedures with us. Wells saw that Samuel was only sixteen, and the beer next to him implied that certain laws had been broken. A second cruiser was called, employing more troops—four altogether, two in each cruiser. Letting Chris go, the cops had cuffed me and Samuel, who were now sitting in separate cruisers.

The cops brought me and Samuel to the station and cuffed only me to a sideways metal bar that stretched along the wall. I was not in a jail cell. I knew this because there was no toilet in the stall and no bars to peer out of, but rather four white walls, an open door parting the wall to my left. There was nowhere to sit in this stall, so I stood, holding my bladder and hearing the cops charge Samuel, who had refused my offering of beer, with possession of alcohol—*one* beer he hadn't even drunk.

"I have to piss!" I slurred loudly and angrily.

"You're going to have to wait!" said a stern voice outside the stall.

"I have to fucking piss!"

"Hold it!" sounded the voice.

"I'll piss in the corner!" I said as I stepped toward the corner, the steel handcuffs banging the bar as they were pulled along with me.

"If you do, we'll charge you with malicious damage to property!"

My fingers on my fly, about to unzip, I stopped myself. Then a cop I'd never met before came into the room, uncuffed me, walked me out of the room, like a dog on a leash, and past Samuel and two police officers and a lady on the opposite side of a counter of some sort and into a jail cell, where I unzipped my pants and, holding my penis, pointing it diagonally at the toilet, relieved myself.

I sighed.

When I'd finished, the unfamiliar cop brought me back to the empty room, bracing me to the metal bar again.

SO WHY IS MY EYE *black?* I wonder.

"Oh yea," I say. "I was hit in the face with a WET FLOOR sign."

"At least," the manager says, "it wasn't a DRY FLOOR sign."

Leftists on Display

A short story….

"… each and every one of them dressed from head to toe in tie-dye …"

TWO PARALLEL LINES OF LEFTISTS were goose-stepping through the streets, each and every one of them dressed from head to toe in tie-dye, with a pink armband wrapped around their left arms, a baby-blue peace symbol in the center. Their sandals slapped the ground in unisons. With the knife edge of their hands pressed to their hearts they karate-chopped the air, keeping their hands flat, palm down, pointing to the sky, chanting *"SIEG HAIL!"*

My eyes burned with rage as I watched the retched display of peace. Was I the only one who understood the hypocrisy here? My beating heart mimicked the steady drumroll—*thump-thump, thump-thump.* Concealed in the crowd, I pulled the pin and catapulted the smoke grenade and it bounced off the ground. Everyone was quiet at first, watching in amazement as the grenade burst and billows of smoke blinded the onlookers' eyes.

Pandemonium!

I put on my protective goggles and then withdrew my gun. People were screaming, but the gunshots were louder. I took out the drummer boys first. Reloaded. I moved the automatic in a straight line as the bullets, one after another, took down each leftist on display.

By the time the smoke had cleared, I was gone, a job well done.

BACK AT HOME BASE WE discussed a plan of action to liberate the city.

Are you confused?

You see, a liberal institution ceases to be liberal the moment it is established, and that was what we were facing here. Progressive politically-correct men and women had won the war, and it was up to us—the rebellion—to take back our freedoms.

"I say we get them sooner than later," said Sammy.

"How much sooner are we talking about?" Terry said.

"I'm talking about tonight."

Terry rubbed his chin, stroking his beard. "And what do you propose we do to them tonight?" he said.

"We—"

I slammed my hands on the table, and they both glared at me.

"We're going about this all wrong," I said.

"How so?" Terry asked.

"When the attack is meant to happen, it will happen."

Sammy raised his right eyebrow.

"They expect us to come at them organized," I explained. "Well, that's the problem, don't you see?"

"I don't get it," said Sammy.

I smiled and said, "We wait."

"What do you mean, 'We wait'?"

"I mean, we go about what we've already been doing."

"As in, we continue to spread the message of hate?" Terry said.

"Exactly."

"This is preposterous," Sammy said. "We need to act, and we need to act now."

"We're already acting. We continue to be dicks, is basically what I'm saying. We do everything in our power to piss them off, and they'll come after us."

"But why wait for them to act?"

"Because," Terry said "—don't you get it?—they want us to be established. That way they win. We are fighting for freedom, correct?"

Sammy nodded.

"Okay, then, don't you see? Being a dick is the ultimate freedom. We need to exercise our right to be dicks."

"Yes, Terry," I said, "you get it. We need to be as uncouth as possible and throw their PC in their faces. PC is the enemy of freedom."

"Okay," Sammy said. "So by saying that we need to be dicks you're being ironic, because the answer is acting as crude, rude, and lewd as possible? Just throw our middle fingers in the air, is what you're saying?"

"Exactly."

My Fear of Spiders

A personal essay....

"... and with me still holding the button the spray would slam the spider into the wall and I would continuously blast the spider with the lethal liquid ..."

JEREMY IS NOT AFRAID OF *anything,* Zack said; *well, except for spiders*. This conversation took place in Dorchester, MA, an inner city of Boston, in Karl's backyard after we'd blown a bundle of coke. What had provoked Zack's saying this was my taunting the car full of black girls in the parking lot we had had to cut through to get to Karl's apartment, where, as I have said, we had gotten cranked on coke, and were now sitting outside and Zack had made the claim that except for spiders I am fearless. Let us explore this notion.

Those creepy crawling little monsters will sneak up on you when you least expect it. You cannot run, you cannot hide. They are everywhere,

SPINNING WEBS!!!

Spiders are absolutely horrid. My last apartment was infested with big nasty barn spiders. They liked to hang out in the bathroom. Every time I went to take a shower, I crept cautiously through the door, a bottle of RAID Hornet/Wasp Killer in my hand, held as if it was a gun, my finger on the trigger, and the moment I saw a spider I drowned the retched thing in that scornful spray. What would happen, I would creep through the door slowly, keeping the RAID trained on the corners, see a spider, then jerk the spray bottle so it was aimed at the monster, and a stream would surge out and hit the horrid creature so hard that it would fly five feet through the air, and with me still holding the button the spray would slam the spider into the wall and I would continuously blast the spider with the lethal liquid for such a long time that it would eventually drown in a sea of toxins.

One night while in bed I heard my cat outside crying to be let in. I sprang up and went to the door. When I stepped out into the hall a black dot the size of a baseball came at me, and when I noticed all eight black legs scurrying across the carpet, I jumped back into my apartment like a little school girl and braced the door with my back. I held the door, almost expecting the furry beast to beat the door in an effort to break in. After some time went by, I grabbed the RAID off the coffee table, and gulped while gripping the door handle, bracing myself for what was out there. My face was itchy with sweat, and for a moment I thought there were spiders all over me. I jumped again, flailing my arms, and if my windows were open I would have been quite embarrassed. There were no spiders on me. I quickly swung the door open and there, on the floor, stood the furry black beast. I aimed the spray and a stream hit the spider, and it ran away, the spray staying locked on as it went. I probably sprayed that thing for five minutes or so.

The following night Dianne stayed over, and while we watched a movie, another big black spider showed itself—though I am convinced that the latter and the former spider were one and the same. I sprayed it with the RAID, and it disappeared behind my desk. After about ten minutes or so, it showed itself again, the raid having done nothing. Dianne hopped the coffee table and swiped the stapler off the floor and slammed it down on the spider—my savior.

However, it has been a while since I have seen a spider in my apartment. I think they are as scared of me as I am of them. They are scared of drowning in RAID, because they know that that is their fate.

When I first moved in, there were spiders everywhere, webs suspended where the ceiling meets the walls, and I would have my friends come over and wipe away the webs with my feather duster. I will not go near a web, not even a cobweb that has been vacant for days, weeks, or even months. Years. Decades. Centuries or millenniums. I mean, what if there is a spider hidden somewhere in the web waiting for me and the moment I brush the duster along the wall, it jumps on me, landing on my face, and stabs me with its protruding fangs, puncturing my skin, and injects its venom into my bloodstream? That would be awful, so I sacrifice my friends for the cause.

I know that spiders do not actually have it in them to drive their teeth into me, but knowing is only half the battle. Most spiders I see are not even lethal. That is why I have no qualms about sending my friends in to fight the spiders. But I, on the other hand, am arachnaphobic. That the bite will not kill me does not ease my mind, because the irrational fear is sure to give me a heart attack and I will fall on the floor, with my arms and legs flailing like those of a spastic.

My fear of spiders, I think, comes from karma. I loved bugs and insects when I was a little kid. I once found an ant that could swim, and I named it Jaws, because, not only could it swim, it was big and tough. I recall it fighting a beetle and winning. I loved that ant for the whole four hours before I accidentally, sadly, suffocated it by keeping it locked up in a box so it would not run off on me.

I had had this friend named Bryan, a midget, and he, too, had loved bugs. He assisted me in running a water hose through a big beehive hanging in my backyard. Even though he was a midget and his legs were shorter than mine he outran me, somehow, and later I was rushed to the hospital because I was allegedly allergic to bees and my whole arm had swelled up like a water balloon. After certain tests were done, the doctors decided I was not allergic to bees, but that I had just been stung by so many bees in such close quarters.

Another fun activity I had partaken in as a kid was pulling the legs off Daddy Long Legs and watching them grow back. But today if I were to see a Daddy Long Leg anywhere near me I am likely to shriek, curling up my knuckles and holding them at my chest, my feat bouncing up and down as if jogging in place.

That I tortured helpless bugs and insects might be one reason why I am scared of spiders, because, for the fear, I know, is irrational, I feel as if the spiders are out for revenge. Another reason I thought of is that my brother had been bitten by three spiders on his arm while he slept one night, and had to go to the hospital the next day, and it was at that point in life when I think my phobia had first become prevalent.

I remember this one night when Theo and I were tripping on Triple C's and halfway into the night a big barn spider, suspended upon the wall, descended its web, scaring the crap out of us, and we had come up with a theory—although half-baked—that spiders can sense when you are tripping, and they wait for that time to come so they can drop down on you and nobody will believe a word you say because although you're telling the truth that spiders are smart and eerily clever, you were tripping when it happened and nobody believes a drug addict.

Spiders *do* know what they are doing, and do not turn your back because, for all you know, you will be their next victim.

Edgar

A short story….

"… during which the two of them got very very drunk, the following hours feeling like a blur …"

Play>

KAT HURRIED ALONG THE CROWDED streets, passing hobos and prostitutes, drug dealers and pimps. *"Street walkers,"* the wealthy would call them. *"Trash."* That was what they were worth.

"Hey, you wanna get high?" a dirty man said as Kat scurried past. "Don't ignore me," he said to her back as she continued moving, hanging her head and hugging her red coat closed.

"Bitch, the man's talkin' to you," another street walker said.

She just continued walking, keeping her head down.

"Lookin' for a good time?" a woman's voice purred, and Kat grimaced, not looking up once.

"Yea, lookin' for a good time?"—a man's voice. She finally looked forward, and a naked man was holding open his trench coat, flashing his hairy pecker. Wincing, she looked back at her feet. She rushed past him.

Then she pushed through a crowd of people huddled around a door. She pushed through the door. She entered the smoky bar she had gotten to know well in the past few days. She hurried past the bar.

"Hey, there's a one drink minimum, miss," the bartender bellowed.

"I'm here to see Edgar," she said, not stopping.

"She's here to see Edgar," he announced. "Leave her alone."

Then a path cleared up, and she made her way through.

In the far corner she slid into the booth, facing a hooded figure.

"Where's my son?" she asked him.

STOP!

<<Rewind

STOP!

Play>

HE WAS SEATED AT HIS usual table in the back corner of his favorite bar, with clouds of smoke idling in the rancid air. It was dark in the bar, and the beer, which Edgar lifted to his lips and poured in his mouth, tasted even worse than the terrible lingering smell. He liked it, though. No. No, he loved it—the more terrible the taste, the better the buzz. He especially loved the beer served at this bar—911, it was called, named after the old emergency hotline that had shut down a few years back.

This story starts inside 911.

A boy with a hood flipped over his head to hide his face slid into the booth across from Edgar.

Edgar nodded and said, "Brian."

"Edgar," Brian returned. He removed his hood, revealing an acne-covered face. It wasn't a pretty sight, but Brian had accepted it *as his own.*

"Can I help you?"

Brian looked around, scanning for suspicious people. He glanced past the bar, then turned back to Edgar. "How's your money situation?"

"How's yours?" Edgar knew the boy was no good. He was a con artist. He was trouble, more trouble than Edgar wanted to deal with right now, for he only wanted to drink his drink and leave.

"It could be better. Now, you never answered *my* question. How's *your* bank account looking these days?"

"Who wants to know?"

"I know of a woman who could," Brian lowered his voice to a whisper, "use your assistance, if you catch my drift."

"I'm listening."

Brian looked over to the bar again. "Hey, bartender," he shouted.

The bartender returned his gaze, with an expression of annoyance plastered to his face.

"A round of your finest," Brian said.

Edgar just barely saw the bartender nod his head, but he did see it, nonetheless.

Brian turned back to Edgar. "Meet me here tomorrow," he said all-hush-hush. "Same time, same place. And," he raised his voice to a regular volume, "as for now—"

A gorgeous woman wearing a sexy white uniform arrived with a tray topped with two glasses of beer, foam spilling over the tops. Edgar could tell Brian was annoyed by the interruption, but oh well, because: *Beer, beer, we want more beer,* Edgar chanted to himself as they each took a beer from the tray. *All the lads are cheerin', get the fuckin' beer in.* The waitress walked away as he continued the chant: *Beer, beer, we want more beer. Now!*

Brian held his beer in the air. "As for now," he said, "we sit back and enjoy. To money," he added.

"To money," Edgar mimicked.

They *clink*ed their glasses together, initiating the night ahead, during which the two of them got very very drunk, the following hours feeling like a blur. They told tales of mischief, Brian doing most of the talking, showing off his bad self, with Edgar humoring him, laughing at the hedonistic tales of self-claimed courage and stupidity—mostly stupidity, though. In fact, they were mostly stupid *and* cowardly, very cowardly. But from the proper perspective they did, however, sound quite courageous. Brian did know how to tell a tale; he sure could spin a story.

Soon the sun came up, and the next day passed as Edgar worked his ass off to find food by doing what he did best. He hustled, he cheated, he lied, and he stole, though he didn't accomplish too much in the course of the day. He did have his good days, but, unfortunately, he had his bad days too, and today was one of his bad days.

By nightfall it had begun to rain. Edgar could hear the heavy drumming on the roof of 911. It was a slow night there. There were two men standing by the bar, one waitress on duty, the bartender, and then there was Edgar, seated in the back corner. The door *bang*ed against the wall, and Edgar peered out of his booth, checking if it was Brian, but it wasn't. It was a well-dressed man carrying an umbrella. Edgar sighed.

On the table before him sat a glass of beer that he had spent his last few dollars on. Hopefully the job with which Brian was setting him up would pay well, because he sure could use the money. He lifted the beer to his lips and poured it in, then was surprised to see Brian sitting across from him when he set the drink down. He had come out of nowhere. However, that was typical of Brian; a real sneaky bastard, he was.

"Where is she?" Edgar said.

"She'll be here. Relax." As he said that, the door *bang*ed against the wall again, and they both peeked out of the booth to see a woman wearing a red rain coat coming their way. "That's her," Brian said.

The woman had long luscious legs wrapped in red stockings that stuck out from under her coat, carrying her beautiful body to the back corner of the bar. Brian moved over to make room as she slid in beside him.

"Edgar," Brian said. "I'd like you to meet Kat."

"Pleasure to meet you," Edgar said, offering his hand over the table.

Kat took his hand. "The pleasure's all mine," she said soothingly and seductively, and Edgar quivered at the sound.

"How can I help you?"

She tossed a bundle of bills held together with a money clip onto the table. "Two men have taken my son, and they expect a large pay off." The seduction in her voice had turned to worry. "They want me to pay two grand, and I'm offering you five hundred to handle it."

"Five hundred?" Edgar smirked. "One grand."

"Pardon me?"

"I said I won't do it for any less than one grand."

She thought for a moment. "Seven-hundred-fifty?" she offered.

"One grand."

The same waitress from the day before appeared with a tray topped with two beers. Edgar and Brian each took one.

"I took the liberty," Brian said, "of ordering us each a drink."

Edgar didn't thank him, because he was too busy watching the sexy waitress's ass wave goodbye, weaving back and forth, as she strode back to the bar.

Edgar snapped out of the trance and noticed there were only two beers but there were three of them. "What about Kat?" he said. "She doesn't drink?" It was as if she wasn't even there, Edgar referring to her in third person.

"No, she doesn't," Brian said.

Edgar leaned forward and looked right into Kat's gorgeous green eyes. "You don't drink?" he asked her.

She shook her head.

Edgar nodded. *Who doesn't drink?* He downed his drink in one gulp before turning to leave.

"Please," Kat said. "Stop."

Edgar did, and glanced at her. "Quit wasting my time."

"Seven-hundred-fifty is all I got."

He looked at her wrist, zeroing in on her Rolex. "I'm sure that's not true."

Looking down at her lap, she pouted. "Okay," she said. "One grand."

"I didn't quite catch that."

"I said"—a hint of irritation in her voice—"okay, I'll do it." Reluctantly she tossed another bundle onto the table, and Edgar smiled at the sight.

"That's seven-hundred-fifty. I'll give you the rest when I get my son back."

Edgar nodded, knowing well that she'd intended to pay him seven-hundred-fifty dollars all along—why else would she have seven-hundred-fifty dollars all bundled up like that? He picked up the first bundle and then skimmed through it as if it were a moving picture book. He did the same with the second, slightly smaller bundle. All the money was there.

Edgar said, "You have a cell?"

"Yes," said Kat. "I do."

"Then arrange a meeting, and we'll meet them there."

STOP!

Fast Forward>>

STOP!

Play>

THEY ARRANGED TO MEET THE kidnappers in an abandoned impound lot, where Daniel and his partner Peter guarded a young boy, whose hands were tied behind his back and his feet to the chair in which he was seated.

Daniel wielded a double-barrel sawed-off shotgun, and Peter a mini Uzi.

From a block away Edgar watched them via binoculars through a third-story window. He had climbed the fire escape and then broken in to the apartment by smashing the window with his crowbar. Edgar was keeping a vigilante eye on the two men whom he recognized as a couple of local thugs, and who both held heavy artillery while Edgar only had a crowbar and his own wits. He had to come up with a plan. And quick!

The rain had stopped, but the ground was still wet. The moon was full, its beaming bright light illuminating the two kidnappers and their hostage. In the distance beyond the lot was the ocean, the savage seesawing waves overtaking the shore like a band of pirates commandeering a vessel. Edgar could hear the thrashing waves as he crept through the dark shadows, searching for the right vantage point for an ambush. He was listening as Daniel asked Peter, "What time is it?"

"Four-fourteen a.m.," said Peter.

"I thought," Daniel said, "she said she'd meet us here at four."

"She did."

Bingo!—Edgar found the perfect vantage point. Time to take his plan into action.

He crouched behind the car. Then he *bang*ed the crowbar, hard, on the steel fender three times.

"What was that?" Edgar heard Peter say.

"Go check on it," said Daniel.

Peter started toward the sound, his footsteps splashing in the puddles leftover from the rain. As his footsteps grew in volume, getting closer to Edgar, getting louder, Edgar somersaulted to another car, over which he peered, watching Peter until Peter was standing by the former car Edgar had hidden behind. As if on cue, Edgar stood up silently. He allowed the crowbar to slip down his forearm, and caught it before it hit the ground, the hook end hanging. Then, like a pole-vaulter, he hopped over the hood, arching his back while in motion. Perfectly he landed on his feet, deserving of a drumroll, though the only problem was: *he was standing in a puddle,* having splashed in it. He would have bowed if it hadn't been for that puddle. As his fight-or-flight instincts kicked in, he swore under his breath, knowing Peter must have heard him.

And he had, because he was craning his head.

As Peter did so, his feet firmly planted, Edgar, having to act *right fucking now,* attacked, whipping the crowbar like a grappling hook before Peter had time to react. The hook caught Peter's left leg, robbing him of his balance, his arms and legs flailing as he flopped on his back, the Uzi firing a three-round burst. Then Edgar drove the bar down on Peter's dome; his flailing limbs went limp on impact. He lay in the shadows unconscious, possibly even dead. Edgar retrieved Peter's right wrist and checked his pulse. Still alive. He bashed Peter's face with his elbow until Peter's uneven breathing stopped. Checked his pulse again. Dead.

Meanwhile, alerted by the gunshots, Daniel's guard was up, and he was waving the shotgun. "Peter!" he called out.

No answer.

"Peter!" he called out again.

Bang!—it came from behind.

He turned quickly.

No one was there.

He dropped down to one knee, then with his knife started to saw the rope that held the boy. He cut the rope holding the boy's legs. Then, with his hands still tied, Daniel hoisted the boy up onto his shoulder, with one hand securing him there, the other gripping the shotgun. Waving the shotgun like a magic wand to ward off danger, craning his neck to keep a keen look out, Daniel tiptoed toward the exit of the lot.

The shotgun was yanked from his hand, and fired when it hit the ground. In utter shock he looked at the shotgun and some sort of bar lay beside it. He turned toward where the bar had—

—Edgar lunged at him like a lion.

As Daniel fell backwards, the boy slipped loose from his grip and ran, his hands bound together, to the exit, where he stopped to watch the two men wrestling in the dirt, Edgar on top, straddling Daniel. As Edgar cocked his arm back, Daniel cocked his head left so as not to get creamed when Edgar fired his fist, but missed, instead having gunned it into the ground, wincing from the jolt and rattle of the blow. Then Daniel's brass knuckles-encased fist sprang up like the recoil of a spring, smashing Edgar's jaw sideways, his teeth *clack*ing together as one lone tooth chipped and ripped loose, followed by a trail of blood which splattered Daniel's face and stained his shirt. After that Edgar fell to the ground. Daniel mounted him, plowing a knee into his nuts. The unbearable pain surged to Edgar's stomach right before Daniel dispensed a rapid-fire pummeling that consisted of bulldozing and railroading Edgar's face, the brass knuckles breaking teeth and tearing skin. When Daniel finally stopped, staring down into the feeble eyes of his foe, he scrambled to his feet and strolled to the shotgun, taking his time as Edgar lay in the dirt, utterly dull, his beaten face flushed with black-and-blues, wearing blood as if it were makeup. Daniel was almost there when—

—Edgar grabbed his ankle, and he fell flat on his stomach.

Edgar was on Daniel quick, his knee stabbing into Daniel's spine. He grabbed a handful of Daniel's hair, pulled his head back, and bashed him face first one, two, three, four, five times into the ground before spotting the shotgun. He released his grip on Daniel's hair and darted to where the shotgun lay, diving to pick it up. At first Edgar fumbled with the shotgun. But once he had a steady grip he rolled over onto his back. Daniel was only just getting up as Edgar leveled the shotgun to his face. When Daniel lifted his head, now looking down the barrel, both of his hands floated up to the red sky.

BANG!!!

STOP!

Fast Forward>>

STOP!

Play>

IN THE FAR CORNER OF 911, Kat slid into the booth, facing a hooded figure.

"Where's my son?" she asked him.

The hooded figure disrobed, and she saw Brian's pimply face.

"You have the rest of the money?" he said.

Fear hit her, hard. "Where's Edgar?"

"Do you have the rest of the money?"

"Where's Edgar?"

Brian took a swig of his beer, then leaned in, propping his elbow on the table, and threw a cold hard stare her way. He said, very firm, "I'm not going to ask you again." Then produced a crowbar, slamming it on the table's surface, the table's legs rattling.

Eyes wide and jaw agape, she immediately obeyed, tossing a bundle of bills onto the table. Brian picked up the bundle and then skimmed through it just like Edgar had done the day before.

"Do you have my son?"

He smiled at her.

"What's so funny? Do you have my son?"

"It's going to cost you another grand," he said.

"Where's Edgar? I want to talk to Edgar."

"But you can't."

"Why the hell not?"

"He's ensuring the safety of your son."

She sat back in her seat.

"For now, at least."

To Kat it all started to make sense, and tears welled up in her eyes. "But why?" she said. "Why would you do this to me?"

"Because times are hard...."

A Note from Arnold Gold

A short story….

"… an umbrella in one hand, protecting her from the pouring rain, and a bundle of roses in the other …"

TO WHOMEVER THIS MAY CONCERN,

Something happened to me that changed my life, and I would like to deliver to you the same inspiring message that brought me an endless supply of joy. It was miraculous. I do not know the cause of that crazy event, though, but I have a feeling it was God-sent. If that be the case, then I feel obliged to pass it along, hopefully helping out someone else like me, or unlike me too.

It started one hot day in July, with the AC discharging cool air into my room, with the window shades drawn to keep out the sun.

I was sitting on my bed, atop the blue comforter, wondering about death—my death, to be specific—wondering when it would come, for it would come soon. You see, I was seventy-three years young at the time.

Mounted across from me was a mirror, and I watched my reflection mimic me as I lifted the glass of whiskey to my lips, the ice cubes *clink*ing together, and took a sip.

The image in the mirror blurred out of focus. *That's strange,* I thought. I removed my glasses and rubbed my eyes. When I rested my glasses on my nose again, the image was back in focus, only it was not me I was staring at, but rather my twenty-three-year-old self. The image was dressed just like me, its legs crossed just like mine, sipping a glass of whiskey just like me, but when I waved my hand counterclockwise my twenty-three-year-old self did not copy. I then waved my hand clockwise and the man whom I had once known so many years ago just sipped the whiskey, staring back at me, eyes locked.

I stood up and stepped to the glass, wanting desperately to be that man sitting across from me. I got closer to the glass. Reached out and touched the glass. Radiating from my fingers were little ripples of waves. It felt as though I could stick my hand through, but I could not; that was as far as I could go.

"Arnold!" my wife, Wendy, called from downstairs, and her voice was carried through the door.

I reeled in my hand, and the ripples smoothed out to be a solid surface again.

"Arnold!"

"Coming!" I shouted.

I tightened my tie around my neck before turning to go to the door. Rounded the bed and walked to the door. Opened it. On the other side was a graveyard, and it was raining. It was a large field, the grass freshly groomed, and tombstones jutted out of the ground in rows. I watched as a woman cut through the field. An umbrella in one hand, protecting her from the pouring rain, and a bundle of roses in the other. On closer inspection I saw that it was Wendy who was cutting through the field.

What was she doing?

She stopped at a grave and placed down the flowers. I removed my glasses again and rubbed my eyes. When I slid my glasses over my ears, I was looking at the grave as though through binoculars, and engraved in the stone was my name with a date next to it. I could not make out clearly what date it was. Something strange was going on. I watched Wendy mourn her dead husband.

Her dead husband!

I slammed the door shut and it *thump*ed against the wall. When I turned around I saw the smile beaming from my twenty-three-year-old self. I went to the mirror, mesmerized. The image reflecting back at me was in shape, unlike me. Its skin was smooth. Confidence showed on its face, and it did not wear glasses. I moved closer to the mirror and touched the rippling glass again. I pushed, but still could not penetrate the reflection.

That was when I cried, tears trickling from my eyes. I plopped down on my bed and watched the image sip its whiskey. Was I going crazy? I looked at my own hand, then at the whiskey glass on my bedside table, then at the image that was sipping whiskey from a glass.

I could have sworn I saw my twenty-three-year-old self wink at me just then. It was as though I was the reflection, and my twenty-three-year-old self was watching me.

"Arnold!" My wife again. "Arnold! What are you doing?!"

Reluctantly I stood up and went to the door. Grabbed the handle. Gulped, bracing myself for whatever might be behind the door. I twisted the handle and heard a faint *click*. The door opened, and I sighed with relief when the hallway that was supposed to be outside my bedroom was outside my bedroom.

But rounding the corner was a black hooded figure, and all the lights dimmed as it floated toward me, a sickle in its hand. Each light mounted on the wall exploded like a grenade as the figure floated by, and darkness enveloped the hallway.

The figure came closer, its face concealed in darkness. All I could make out were the two bright red eyes that shined from deep inside the dark hood. Its right arm lifted up and a bony albino hand moved toward me, its pointer finger pointed forward, as if trying to touch me.

I slammed the door, and with my back to it, braced the door with all my strength.

The handle twisted left and right as a force pushed the door, trying to break through, but I would not let anything come through, not now after what I had seen; not even would I let Wendy through.

Something pounded on the door—*bang, bang, bang!*

I gulped.

The pounding continued as fear forced its way into my mind, fear of the inevitable future, my inevitable death which was waiting for me outside the safety of my bedroom. The grim reaper had come to reap my soul. Then the pounding stopped.

The handle twisted left and right, *click*ing each time it switched directions. The pressure behind the door was pushing so powerfully that I had to walk backwards to keep the door from bursting open.

More pounding!

"Arnold!" my wife shouted.

Then the pounding stopped.

I could hear footsteps padding the floor, backpedaling down the hall, getting quieter.

Then louder as they descended the staircase, and finally the noise ceased.

For now I was safe. I wiped the sweat from my forehead.

My eyes locked on to the man in the mirror. All the excitement behind the door had made me forget about the familiar face in the mirror. My face, only fifty years younger. I let up on the door and dropped to my knee. Peeked through the keyhole, and the brightly lit hallway was empty. I sighed, then got up. I crept to the mirror and sat down on the bed.

The image blurred.

Then focused.

It was my face I was seeing now. My seventy-three-year-old face. The face had glasses on. The face was wrinkly, just like mine. As relieved as I was to see things back to normal, I felt a feeling of anguish at knowing that this man in the mirror was me, only me, and I would never again be faced with myself from the past. This realization bothered me more than the fact that reality was restored. I reached for the whiskey and downed the glass, drowning my sorrow with drink.

"Arnold!" my wife shouted again.

I stood up and made my way to the door. When the handle was in my hand I stopped, because what if the insanity had not ended? What if the grim reaper was still out there waiting for me? I let go of the handle and stared at it. I could have sworn it was breathing, growing and then shrinking, growing and then shrinking, as if it was taunting me.

"Arnold!"

"What?!" I boomed.

"What are you doing?!"

I flung the door open and in front of me was a brightly lit hallway. The darkness had long gone. But still, what if—? Anything could happen beyond this door.

Anything!

I could not do it. I could not face whatever was out there.

I closed the door. Looked over my shoulder, hoping my twenty-three-year-old self had come back.

But it had not. Could it have just been an illusion? Had I imagined everything that had happened? It had been too real. My imagination was not that good. It could not be. I paced up and down, thinking desperately for a solution.

"Arnold!"

I had to do this. I had to face my fears. I had to leave my bedroom. If I never faced my fears of what might be, I would die a lonely man.

I opened the door, then sighed at the sight of everything as it should be. It was a refreshing sight, but a bit frightening when I glanced at the mirror and it was only me. I stood there staring out in the hallway, my hand still clutching the handle.

Then I let go.

I crossed the threshold and continued. My armpits were sticky with sweat. I ran a hand through my moist hair. The spiral staircase came closer to me, and it felt as though I was not moving but rather very still and the staircase was slowly catching up. I was viewing everything through tunnel vision, focused on my fate which was the staircase that twisted and turned and took me to the bottom floor, where—

I could not believe my eyes.

In the large room at the foot of my staircase, there were people who had gathered here in my house. People sipping scotch. Drinking wine. Beer. Talking to one another. Smiles on their faces. Couples dancing to the easy jazz. It was unbelievable.

I stood there with my eyes lit up and my jaw agape when Wendy came over to me and clutched my shoulder. She led me through the room, and I spotted a pyramid of presents stacked tall on a table. My vision locked on to the table as my legs continued, my neck craning as I passed the pyramid.

As Wendy led me to a long rectangular table dressed in a white cloth, with place settings along the sides and one on either end, a woman who I recalled meeting only once many many years ago greeted me with a warm smile and very pleasantly said, “Happy birthday.”

I continued past her to one end of the table and sat down in my designated seat. I sat there for a while, with my head hung down, my mind still in my bedroom.

I then heard the *ding-ding-ding* of a knife tapping a wine glass, and when I looked up, I saw someone whose name I did not recall standing up by the table. When the room quieted and the music muted, he started droning on and on about how close he and I were and about how great of a gentleman I was. But I could not tell you exactly what he said, because my mind was not receiving in this room. My mind had left my head and was still upstairs.

The only thing I did catch of his toast was "Happy seventy-fourth birthday."

Which brought me back to reality. I looked all around me and saw a room filled with joyous faces. I was not joyful, though. Why was I not joyful?

When more guests took turns standing up to make toasts in my honor, I just mulled over this whole night and realized there was so much I had not done. I would die soon, that was for sure, but I did not want to die unfulfilled. Maybe this night was my wakeup call, a sign saying that I had to take some actions. I really did not know what this all meant. Either way, though, as I sat listening to these strangers reminisce about the past, about my past of which they had not been apart, about which they knew nothing, about which they had only been told by my selfish wife who had only invited her friends to this celebration in my honor, I decided I would first divorce Wendy and then disappear on an extraordinary adventure, maybe go skydiving or hike Mount Washington or windsurf or even just surf.

I would fulfill my longing before I died, and looking back on it now while lying in a hospital bed, with tubes protruding from holes in my skin, I think I can honestly say I have no regrets. I set things right in my life.

So I hope this note inspires you to have no fears and take life by its leash and live out your dreams.

Good luck,
Arnold Gold

Nothing I Stand For

A personal essay....

"... 'I know, but what's the point?' ..."

IF EVERYTHING IS NOTHING, NOTHING *has* to be everything. No, wait, that doesn't make any sense. But it doesn't have to make sense. Does anything make sense? No. It just is what it is. And until you are ready to accept life's paradox you will suffer.

Or you could also be ignorant. Ignorance, they say, is bliss.

Things happen because they happen; not because they have any higher calling.

I was getting down on myself one day, melancholy. Chuck, the guitarist of my old band, Lethal Erection, asked me if I wanted to have a band practice.

Feeling hopeless, I asked Chuck, "But what's the point?

"To practice," he replied.

"I know, but what's the point?"

"To practice."

"I know, but what's the point?"

"To practice." This went on for close to five minutes. The point of practicing was nothing else but to practice. It was what it was. There was no higher purpose, as much as I wanted there to be. I was having trouble accepting there was no point; therefore, I was afflicted, lost.

The Buddhists say life is suffering—the first noble truth. What causes suffering? The second noble truth explains it all: attachments—we as human beings become attached to things outside ourselves, and when what we are attached to gets taken away, we wish it back, afflicting suffering upon ourselves. When you take away a baby's bottle, what does the baby do? It cries. If the baby was never given the bottle, it would not know what it was missing. I love Kristen. Without her around I miss her; I'm sad because I want her, but I can't have her: she lives too far away. Even when I was living in Boston there were times I could not see her and missed her. I wish I never met her so I would not miss her, so I would have never experienced love. (Ignorance is bliss.)

Acceptance is the key.

The third noble truth: with practice we can put an end to cravings. The fourth noble truth: the end of cravings. What a load of shit! Nobody can end their cravings. The answer is acceptance. One must accept their suffering, then as a result will suffer less. It's a paradox:

Life sucks, but what can I do about it? *Nothing*.

Life is suffering.

The first noble truth.

I think I finally understand.

The key to happiness is a paradox.

One could be happily incarcerated.

The key to happiness.

I figured it out.

Life sucks; get a helmet.

I could endure as much physical pain as you throw at me. If that's so, why can't I endure mental pain?

I figured it out.

When I take a punch I absorb the pain; I let myself really feel the pain, because I know no matter what, the pain will surface. When I accept the pain it goes away.

Life is suffering. Acceptance is the key. If one can accept their own suffering, one suffers no longer.

I'm fucked.

The first noble truth.

When I accept that I'm fucked, I no longer feel fucked. I start to wonder—*this place ain't so bad after all.*

I think I had a moment of clarity.

I'm happy to suffer. I am okay with being fucked. I will always be miserable, but that's okay.

Hope is dead.

Nothing matters.

We are all going to die, but first we will live, and it's what we do when we are alive that matters.

Did I say nothing matters? I meant, everything matters.

EVERYTHING.

It's not that everything is right, but we have the right to do everything. I do not care for subjectivism—the moral theory believing everything we do is right because we feel it is right. That's not right. It can't be right. If everyone is right, then someone must be wrong, but who?

There cannot be right without wrong, good without bad. God *needs* the Devil. Heaven *needs* Hell.

I do not actually believe in Heaven or Hell, God or the Devil. I don't believe in right and wrong. Our actions shouldn't be given labels like that.

People used to say I didn't take responsibility for my actions, but I always took responsibility; I just refused to give my actions value.

Everything is equal.

We act out of necessity and desire. Is it wrong to steal when you are hungry? Or is it right? It's neither. Someone will get hurt either way. Either you remain hungry, or the store loses money. Is it right for the store to let you starve when it has the means of feeding you?

Utilitarianism is the moral theory believing *good* is what promotes the most happiness. Is a starving child a happy child?

Every action has a reaction. Some reactions are desirable; some are not.

Enforcing what is right and wrong is like playing God; no different than murder. Who are we? What makes us so special?

The moral of my story: null and void.

Think for yourself.

THINK!

Think, think, think, don't drink! THINK!

Ask questions.

THINK!

Free will. Use it!

Chaos.

Chaos is order.

America.

Iraq.

Chaos, chaos, chaos. Everywhere is in a perpetual state of chaos.

Deal with it.

Punk Rock.

Everything is nothing.

Free will.

Nothing is everything.

Chaos.

The following events are based on reality:

I was walking down the street, clad in Punk rock attire. Across the street I saw a man wearing Preppy attire. He looked ridiculous. I wanted to stomp his face. He had the right to dress that way; I had the right to smash him, but I waited.

"Freak!" I heard him yell.

"What you say?" I asked loudly enough so he could hear me from across the street. I began walking in his direction. Cars honked at me because I did not look both ways. I was angry. I didn't care. I was fixated on him.

"I called you a *freak*." There was no need for that. He was the freak. We were both freaks, for fuck's sake.

I approached him. We were face to face. Our noses almost touched. Our eyes were parallel. He pushed me with both hands. I raised my hands like a boxer, and spread my feet into a boxer's stance. I swung my clenched fist. He moved his arms to block. Unexpectedly, I kicked him in the nuts. Now he was holding his groin in agony, bent over. I punched him in the face twice, knocking him over. On the ground I kicked him in the head, then I walked away.

Every action has a reaction.

People can do what they want.

Free will.

THINK!

Chaos.

With chaos comes responsibility.
Acceptance is the key.
Acceptance is the end.

Love and Destruction

A short story….

"… but the gesture still deeply penetrated my heart, leaving a permanent hole, in which a safety pin still lingers …"

Chapter 1: Friday Night

IT WAS FRIDAY NIGHT. ENSCONCED in my long faded-yellow couch, devouring a slice of Digiorno pizza, I watched *Spongebob Squarepants,* fully Jaded (nothing fazed me; well, I recognized the humor, but I just couldn't laugh; I mean, why would I laugh? what would be the point?), waiting for the man, and [**knock, knock!**] someone was at my door [**knock, knock!**]—the man, I suspected. A ghostly smile smacked me in the face. I stood up. Then I opened the door heedlessly, knowing precisely who it was: Mikey—tall, thin, short blond hair. We established the deal ["Twenty dollars," he said], quick and easy—I slipped him a ten-dollar bill and two fives and he surrendered a small Ziploc bag complete with two orange hexagonal pills—and then he vanished into the night. I locked the door behind him. Ecstatic, I was.

I broke into the bag hurriedly, like a child on Christmas morning, displaced one pill, and carefully planted the orange hexagon beneath my tongue. The tablet tasted like orange cough syrup—some deem that gross, but I had no complaints. I sat down on my couch and watched *The Fairly*

Odd Parents. The hard part was over. I possessed the drugs, and now I waited for them to kick in. *Waiting*, I thought, *sucks*! I hated time: when I enjoyed myself, time of course cruised by, probably because I paid little attention to the clock. But when I was bored, time lasted forever. I wished I could control time: stop the clock for those rare fun occasions and speed up the clock when boredom struck.

Thirty long boring minutes and one episode of *The Fairly Odd Parents* later, immediately after the first tablet had dissolved, the sickening sweet orange taste still lingering, I inserted the second suboxone beneath my tongue. A queasy feeling slightly upset my stomach, but I managed to hold down any chance of vomit. I lit a cigarette, bored. The pill dissolved after thirty long minutes, although not as long as the last thirty minutes because a sort of numbness had overtaken my senses fifteen minutes ago.

An hour passed ... and I felt numb. I walked over to my computer and played "Run Run Run" by the Velvet Underground: a somewhat fast drum beat escaped from the speakers and a redundant melancholy guitar riff repeated over and over again and a second guitar screeched like grinding metal and I felt compelled to bob my head in time with the beat. I was seated in front of my computer, bobbing my empty head mechanically, sweat plastered to my face ["Run, run, run, run, run...." Lou Reed sang].

The song ended, and I felt accomplished, like I had completed my goal, so I walked to my couch and sat down, tuned in to my TV, which had been left on all the time, pen and notebook in hand, planning an all-nighter. It's almost impossible to sleep on suboxone. I might nod my head, but

... um ... I lost my train of thought. The drugs were kicking in—taking over.

AN HOUR FLIES BY AND *then two hours and I walk, float, from my couch to the other end of my room just for the point and I feel,* how can I describe it? I can't, *phenomenal, I guess, because walking or floating, I guess one could call it, is ÜBER fantastic and bone chilling and this is excellent and I step into the bathroom and aim my limp member down at the toilet and wait and wait and wait and nothing happens because my bladder is too numb and then I gaze into the mirror and my pupils are microscopic—needle-thin—and I look like a star as sweat leaks from every orifice and then I use the sweat to spike my hair and then I look really good and feel even better and then I wander into my room where I locate,* where did I leave them? *my sunglasses and pick them up and slide them over my ears and in front of my eyes and now I'm back in the bathroom and blankly staring into the mirror mesmerized because the most beautiful thing in the world is the mirror and then I gaze up and down my body and I'm wearing a tight red T-shirt and tight blue jeans and I need to gain some weight or muscle because I'm skin and bone and I crave soda,* Mmmm, soda! *and then I leave the bathroom and walk to the door and then I open my front door and step outside and my body quivers with delight because the warm winter wind gently brushes against my body and a euphoric fright swoops through my veins like stepping out into the cold after a long and hard work-out drenched in sweat from the previous hour spent running on the treadmill and I stand at the top of my stoop and hold my head up high and enjoy* *the now and I don't want this moment to end but the inevitable is only seconds away and I feel good and I feel great and I feel—*

I venture to the end of my lot and try not to slip on the ice but lose my balance as I reach the street and I stumble over but catch myself before smacking the pavement and now I'm leaning forward with my feet spread apart forming a triangle the most stable shape in the world and I wipe the sweat from my forehead, That was a close one, *and then pick myself up and stroll down to Walmart and as I arrive at Walmart I stroll through the electric sliding doors and my sunglasses shield my eyes from the bright light in the store and then I scan the store and shift my head left and right like an owl taking everything in and people traipse up and down the aisles and I feel bad for these drones because they're not me and boy does it feel good to be me and then I buy an orange Fanta and a Red Bull and leave,* The cashier must have thought I'm a freak, wearing what I'm wearing, *and then I make it home where I take refuge on the couch and then encompass the TV remote and I point it at the TV and [**click**] the channel changes and I gaze mindlessly at the TV screen and watch reruns of Family Guy and smoke a cigarette ... and then another ... and then another ... and then another as I laugh at the silly antics on TV and then an hour escapes and I'm bored so I slap myself in the face although I knew I would feel nothing and then giggle and enjoy my high and what a wonderful high it is and then I take a swig from my Fanta and then I think of Rebecca,* Sweet sweet Rebecca, I miss her, I really do, how did I manage two and a half years without her? I don't know, *and I recall what Tina told me,* Email her, *so I sit by my computer and log into my* *email account and ... and ... suddenly ... everything fades to black ... and then I lift my head,* Not now, *and I feel tired and worn out and my room is dark the only light shining from my computer screen and I'm seated comfortably in my chair although the hard wood chafes my bony ass and then I nod my head a little but jolt myself back awake and then I look up at the empty screen and type—*

Hi, how are you?

—and I'm seated in my chair eyes on the screen, What should I write next? *and my chin rests on my palm and I figured it out so I move my hands to the keyboard and ready my fingers to type and ... and everything fades to black ... and then sometime later I raise my head and stabilize my head resting my chin on my palm and I need to stay awake my eyes fixated on the screen so I reach for the Red Bull on my desk and chug-a-lug half the can and I set it back on my desk and then check the time—one-o'clock a.m.—*Okay, I can do this, *and then I debate what I should write next because I haven't seen Rebecca in two years so this email has to be flawless—*

Hi, how are you?

I haven't seen you in close to two years, and I still think about you all the time.

—and it's perfect and ... and everything fades to black ... and then I raise my head struggling to keep my eyes open and then type—

> Hi, how are you?
>
> I haven't seen you in close to two years, and I still think about you all the time. I've been in treatment for the past year, and I'm doing a lot better than I was.

—No, that's not right: "I've been in treatment for the past year...." Garbage, *and I press backspace deleting the last sentence,* Fuck, what should I write next? *... and ... and everything fades to black ... and I raise my head and I have to stop nodding off so I kill my Red Bull and fling it toward the trash can across the room missing by about five feet and then notice the time—three-twenty-four a.m.,* I was out for a while—*and I conclude my email—*

> Hi, how are you?
>
> I haven't seen you in close to two years, and I still think about you all the time.
>
> Guess what? I'm sober!
>
> I really miss you. I talked to Tina, and she said you're sober and doing a lot better than you were. So I was hoping we could talk and maybe see each other in the near future.

—and then I nod my head ... and I drift ... away ... letting ... the ... do ... pe ... t ... a ... k ... e ... over.

Chapter 2: Rebecca and I

A WEEK LATER I FOUND myself seated at a large wooden desk in a bright-lit room, four white walls on each side, an open door parting the wall to my right. Another desk, on which a wide flat-screen computer was perched in the right corner, stood perpendicular to mine. I still felt the büpe I had taken the night before, like a manic euphoria had overtaken my senses hours earlier and **still** kicked my ass. My nerves ran haywire, sending foggy messages to my brain. Expectantly, a tall pudgy Irishman wearing a green scaly cap walked into the room carrying a clear plastic rectangular box with a white lid, and set the box in front of me ["How's everything going?" he asked]. He sat down at the other desk ["All right," I lied]. I was better than all right [I asked: "You?"]. Sweat leaked from every pore in my face. Four drawers were stacked vertically beneath the computer—stacked from the floor up ["Better than yesterday," he replied. "I was terribly sick"]. Alan, the Irishman, opened the top drawer ["I figured," I said. "I didn't see you all day yesterday, so I thought, he's probably sick"], from which he revealed a plastic bag containing a clear plastic cup [then asked: "You got any piss inside you?" / "Possibly"], and handed me the bag ["You know the drill"], which I took from him ["I'll see what I can do," I said, a tad bit nervous].

I left the room briskly, feeling supreme and energized, ready for anything thrown my way. I was supposed to urinate in the cup to prove I hadn't used any drugs. Which I hadn't, of course. None that anyone would know about, anyone other than me. I got tested for opioids, but suboxone is artificial. Nobody would know. Except for me, of course. I was golden, I must say. How it worked:

suboxone contains an opiate blocker. I wouldn't have felt so supreme if it blocked the drug that got me high. That wouldn't make any sense. So, suboxone is artificial; Alan had no clue about this active drug in my system. He **could** test for it if he only knew, but he didn't, therefore I was golden.

Standing in the bathroom facing the toilet, pointing my limp member into the cup, I squeezed my bladder with all my power. Nothing. My bladder was still numb. *Goddammit, I've had to piss since last night, and still nothing*. I relaxed my bladder for a moment. Then I was at it again, pushing with even more force. Nothing. I reached over to the sink beside myself, turned the left nob counterclockwise, releasing the spray of water. Then slightly clockwise, easing the spray to a drip [**drip, drop! drip, drop!**]. The water dripped out of the faucet, stirring my bladder. I tried again, squeezing my bladder forcefully, but nothing, nothing, nothing came out of my fucking **cock**. I took a deep breath [**inhale**], then let it all out [**exhale**]. Again—*aaaaaaaaaaahhhhh!* Nothing. *What the fuck am I doing wrong?* I devised an abstract approach. Something new; something different. I squeezed my bladder, this time lightly, and I felt a liberating emphatic pressure ease its way into my penis. *It has worked*. But the solace rushed back inside, like a syphon hose released before the discharge pours out. I relaxed my bladder. *Fucking, hell!* I closed my eyes, attempting relaxation, meditation; waterfalls haunted my every thought. I tried once more. The familiar pressure passed through my bladder and into my dick, this time farther, closer, making progress, but, ***fuck me***, was sucked back inside. I tried again ... and ... and ...

and ... nothing. Again ... and ... and ... and ... nothing. Again ... and ... and ... and—

Suddenly a stream of bright-yellow liquid strongly, fluently rushed out of my penis, like a running water hose, and splashed violently as it hit the bottom of the clear cup. I occupied an eighth of the cup, which was enough for a proper urine analysis. I twisted the cap on top of the cup snugly, didn't bother to wash my hands, and then exited the bathroom. As I left the bathroom it hit me: *the lights*. I switched off the lights.

I walked back into the office, passing the cup to Alan as I sat in the chair at the desk, the transparent box with a white lid on the desk in front of me. Alan was seated in a chair at the desk perpendicular to mine, however facing me. I opened the box, took out a small white tray, and placed the tray on the desk ["So, everything's going well?" Alan asked me / "Things are all right," I answered, "as far as I'm concerned"]. The tray had seven slots (columns, I should call them), one for each day, with the specific day labeled—SUN, MON, TUES, WED, THURS, FRI, and SAT—at the top. I removed seven long thin boxes from my backpack, each with four cabinets labeled MORN, NOON, EVE, and BED. I placed each box in their proper slot (column), then opened the MORN, EVE, and BED cabinets (I didn't take noon meds), preparing to pour my meds—I needed to place my medication in their proper cabinets. I removed seven med bottles, short green cylindrical bottles with white screw-on caps, two of which were filled with Ritalin and Klonopin, and placed them beside the tray. Now the tray sat in between my medication bottles and the transparent box. I was going to place the proper pills in their proper cabinets, and when

I finished with each specific pill I was going to place the bottle back in the box ["Are your bills up to date?" he asked / "I believe so," I lied / after a short pause: "How's your eating been?" / "Averagely, about two meals a day. Sometimes less" / "You really need to be eating three meals a day" / "I know, but I'm always on the move. I just don't seem to have the time. I'm—" / "Why," he cut me off, "don't you have the time?" / "I'm busy." Another lie / "Doing what?" / "I—" / "You don't work. You don't go to school," he barked. "What are you doing with all your time?" / *Getting high*, I refrained from saying / "What do you do all day?" / "I've been thinking a lot about an old girlfriend," I replied / "That's what you've been doing?" / "I sent her an email last week" / "Oh, and what's her name?" / "What do you care?" I sneered / "I **do** care" / "Okay. Well, her name's Rebecca. We went out for about four years, the longest time I've ever had a girlfriend. Our relationship ended when I keyed the fuck out of her car" / "What did you do that for?" / "I'd rather not say" / "And does Rebecca use drugs? / "She used to. She's sober now, is what I heard" / **ring, ring!** / "Hold on one second!" he said / **ring, ring!** / "I have to take this"]. He answered his phone [and said: "Hello? / "..." / "Yea?" / "..." / "Yea, yea. All right." Then to me: "I have to step out"]. The Irishman left the room.

I was alone at last, left to my own devises. The Ritalin bottle sat in front of me, calling my name: *Jay. Jay, I'm all yours. Steal me! Steal me, Jay!* Slowly and hesitantly, I unscrewed the white cap on the twenty-milligrams extended-release Ritalin bottle and quickly glanced out the door to my right, making sure I didn't get caught, but stopped this deceitful act when a light bulb flashed in my head: *What am I doing? A drug is a drug is a drug. Ritalin* ***is*** *a drug. What did I say to Rebecca?* ***I'm sober****. But I'm not sober. What about suboxone? Don't be silly. Suboxone is legal. So is Ritalin if I'm prescribed to it. But who am I kidding,* ***it's not as if I'm shooting heroin****. Fuck it!* I stuck my pointer finger inside the bottle, scraped out one tiny white pill, then dropped the pill in my flannel shirt pocket above my chest and quickly glanced out the door to double-check no one had seen. I was golden. I repeated myself, pocketing yet another pill. I now had forty milligrams of white trash cocaine. I stole another pill, this time without hesitation. And another, adding up to eighty milligrams. I took one last pill, because I didn't wish to overdo it. I had one-hundred milligrams of Ritalin, white trash cocaine, speed, nose candy. I was golden. I was still high from last night and carried one-hundred fucking milligrams of nose candy; what could be better? Thinking, *I might need something for the crash*, I stole three Klonopin and then quickly glanced out the door one last time. I continued pouring my medication, pretending to be the honest boy that I was. *Honest ... that's a good one!*

Alan, just as I had predicted, joined me in the room once again [and said: "So, this Rebecca, how'd you meet her?" / "At a show," I said—

THE LOWER CLASS BRATS PLAYED at the Cambridge Elk's Lodge. Harry had accompanied me to the show. Outside smoking cigarettes, after the first two openers had played, Harry, the more social type, introduced me to a short blond girl he had just met ["Jay," he said, gesturing to the girl, "this is Gabriella. Gabriella," gesturing to me, "Jay"]. Our eyes met. She had beautiful blue eyes, her eyebrows shaved off, replaced with black ink, possibly mascara, very sharp and crisp, very serious. We shook hands ["Nice to meet you," I said]. Her hand was soft and fragile ["Nice to meet you too"]. She looked behind her, out in the distance, probing a group of young Punks, like myself, who were all standing around, talking to one another, smoking cigarettes, drinking obviously concealed forty-ounces [and called out: "Rebecca!"]. I took a drag off of my cigarette, waiting for a response. No climax, no conclusion, what the fuck! I looked at Harry, and he shrugged, like he didn't know what to think ["Rebecca!"]. Was this girl cra—

And then I saw her, a stunningly beautiful creature. She strolled through the crowd, big boots, tight black pants, a painted biker jacket, and her hair ... it was tall; I mean, it stood straight up, like the Statue of Liberty's crown, although her spikes covered her entire head, black as night [nearly drooling, hypnotized by the beauty—**her** beauty—I said: "Hi!" / "This is Rebecca!" Gabriella announced, placing her right hand on Rebecca's shoulder. Then, gesturing to Harry, she added: "This is Harry! And," gesturing to me, "this is ... shit!"]. Gabriella beat her forehead with her left hand, still clinging to Rebecca's shoulder [then asked me, still holding her head: "What's your name again?" / "Jay Terror!"]. Harry smirked at that. Aggravated, I turned and shot him a look of disgust, before I held out my hand, anxious to touch Rebecca, to feel her radiating skin embrace me, to share her warmth, her comfort. Everything happened slowly, in slow motion. I arched my elbow, curving it, bending it, moving my hand upward, closer to

Rebecca. I exposed my hand, stiffening my fingers, ready for contact. Taking my lead, she instantly passed me a Steel Reserve. Not quite what I had expected, but the gesture still deeply penetrated my heart, leaving a permanent hole, in which a safety pin still lingers. I took a swig of the Steel Reserve. Then, bewildered and slightly disappointed, I, for the first time, looked up at her, feeling inadequate, undeserving, like I was unworthy, trying to avoid eye contact because I had already felt the familiar sting of rejection shatter my existence, but her gravity pull was too strong for me to resist. Our eyes met, locking us together, joining our souls, the corners of her lips stretching out, curving upward, devising a stunning emphatic joyous grin—when I realized my newfound feelings were mutual—broadcasting the most magnificent smile I had ever seen, and we drifted away into the realms of nothing, somewhere unexplored, uninhabited, only Rebecca and I, lost in each other's eyes, lost in the depth of love, staring, gazing, gawking, all other activities—movements, sounds, people, et cetera—blocked out, only Rebecca and I, staring, gazing, gawking, lost.... What felt like an eternity had lasted not even a minute. It was love all right. Love at first fright. In the years to come she would tell me she had felt the same way on that amazing night.

—**"HOWEVER," I ADDED, "SHE REMEMBERED** meeting me a couple of weeks prior to the show"]. I dropped my last pill in its proper cabinet. Then I handed the tray to Allan to check that I had filled my medication boxes properly. And I was **golden** ["Is there anything else you need to talk about?" he asked / "I'm good. Thanks" / "I guess we're all set in here, then" / "I guess so," I said, imagining what this gorgeous day would bring]. I left Alan's office. Then I exited the house.

Chapter 3: Yummy!

LATER, AFTER THE SUN HAD set, in front of me, a mirror, topped with an appetizing white powder, was perched on my coffee table. With my ATM card I willed the powder. I shaped the powder; I molded the powder; I scraped it across the mirror. I devised a mogul in the center of the mirror. I was about to pull thin lines from the clump. I scraped one line. Then I scraped the excess powder back into the mogul, like when a skier turns, spraying snow to form a small hill; only I was more careful in pushing the powder back into the mogul, not wanting to waste any fuel. I pulled a second line. *Yummy!* I scraped the excess powder, neatening the surface. A third line. Excess powder. A fourth line. Excess powder. A fifth line. Excess powder. I brushed the card across the mirror, pulling the mogul toward me, leaving a sixth line behind. Excess powder. A seventh line. I had just enough excess powder to form one more short line, which was exactly what I did. I had finished. Seven and a half lines waited to be inhaled. Via a rolled dollar bill I inhaled four lines through my right nostril, blasting the powder straight into my bloodstream. I did the same with the remaining three and a half lines, via my left nostril.

***I'M GU-GU-GU-GOLDEN AND ALL MY** fears and anxieties disperse leaving behind a fictional utopia centered in my apartment and then I look left and then right and* *shake my head manically and frantically ... and insanity!!!* music, MUSIC, music, music, music, I need music, I need frantic fucking noise! *so I stand up and my body quivers and then I take one step forward slowly and cautiously and then another step slowly and even more cautiously and I ... I ... I ... I ...* spray paint! *because I want to either create or destroy something—**ANY**thing—b-e-a-utiful because I'm alive because I'm ALIVE because I'm a-l-i-v-e—alive—and I pick up my backpack and unzip it and then I flip my backpack upside-down dumping out the contents and load it with three cans of spray paint—white, black, and—*

I zip through the aisles of Walmart and buy three Monsters—two Monsters and one extra-strength Monster—because I am the Energizer Bunny and just like myself the Energizer Bunny runs on fuel—battery acid—and speed is my fuel, **Gimme an S! S!!! Gimme a P! P!!! Gimme two Es! E-E!!! Gimme a D! D!!! and what does that spell?! SPEED!!!** and the crowd goes wild, *and now I'm home and I'm logged into my email account and Rebecca has yet to respond so fuck! maybe I should make her a video and jog her memory with my webcam and I think I will play "Safety Pin Stuck in My Heart" by Patrick Fitzgerald and yes! that's a brilliant idea and although I was planning to tag some walls downtown dealing with this Rebecca problem is my number one concern so I bring my computer to my couch and turn on my webcam but don't hit play yet because first I ought to browse through my music folder searching for Patrick Fitzgerald and I find him so [**click!**] I open his folder and am bombarded with three more folders and one song which is "Safety-pin Stuck in My Heart" so [**click, click!**] I double-click and the song begins but I press pause and then I start* *recording with my webcam and restart the song and click play and I sit on my couch while the song plays and the webcam records me doing nothing so boredom hits quickly and I light a cigarette thinking it will make me look cool and I take a drag but* **OH NO!** *I'm not wearing my sunglasses although my long black hair is sticking straight up like the singer of the Screamers or more like Sid Vicious although his hair wasn't as long and I say "wasn't" because sadly Sid Vicious died many many years ago but at least my hair makes me look cool and Rebecca has or at least* ***had*** *the hots for Sid Vicious and what was I looking for again?*

Oh yea! my sunglasses which I left on my makeshift desk which is really just a small table that only has enough space for my laptop and an ashtray and of course my sunglasses and my cigarettes and a lighter and as I walk to the table that I painted black with a paint marker which took me all day to do and then I designed a red swastika on top of the black paint using red Duct tape because I was bored one day and a few days earlier a girl I know wasted all my black Duct tape by covering the entire table with it using the entire roll of Duct tape and covering every inch of the table and giving me a brilliant idea for an art project to do to kill time I carry my computer so I can continue recording my pretty face and I arrive at the table and pick up my sunglasses and put them on and I'm sitting on the couch recording myself smoking a cigarette and wearing pitch-black wrap-around shades and I look cool and the camera eats me up and I can't wait to send this video to Rebecca because she will love it and get a kick out of it and then the song ends so I stop recording and log back into my email account and send the video to Rebecca, Please please

please respond back, I love you, I really do, respond back, please please please, *and now that that's done I'm bored again with nothing to do and wired from the Ritalin so I leave my apartment with three cans of spray paint in my backpack and I head downtown and when I get downtown I walk to the bridge where underneath I spray-paint "Jay Terror Says Fuck Off" and "Fuck Religion Fuck Politics Fuck the Lot of You" which is a song by Chaotic Dischord and then I spray-paint "Fuck Off We Murder" which is a song by GG Allin and then I place the cans of spray paint in my backpack and finish drinking my Snapple iced tea which I forgot to mention I have and I throw the bottle at the side of the bridge and [**crash!**] the glass bottle explodes and I feel accomplished and energized and energized and ENERGIZED and my adrenaline pulsates [as I scream: "**Fuck the world!**" but nobody hears me because it's three in the morning] so I creep out from under the bridge and decide to head home and as I enter my apartment I sit down and encompass my notebook in which I write stuff like "I'm sitting on my couch" and "I'm bored" and "I'm high" and "I think I'll watch some TV" but nothing's on because it's so early in the morning so I write "but nothing's on because it's so early in the morning" and turn on Comedy Central from which I watch infomercials not really paying attention as I write in my journal the infomercials acting as background noise which is retarded of me because I have plenty of music on my computer I realize so I stand up and walk to my computer and decide to play ... um ... um ... um ... um ... um ... the Brassknuckle Boys and the first song to play is "Busted and Disgusted" from the album* American Bastard *and I can relate to this song ["I know I'm busted," comes* *from my computer. "I know I'm disgusted. So don't ask me right now, no, 'cause I don't care to discuss it. I know I'm busted. I know I'm disgusted. I know right now, right now, baby, I can't be trusted"] and then "Boulevard of Broken Dreams" which is also from* American Bastard *... and then "Fighting Poor" plays ... and then "From My Heart" plays which happens to be my favorite as I continue to write.*

Chapter 4: November

BRENDAN, SIXTEEN-YEARS OLD, HAD COME home from rehab for a weekend pass. I know it was weird that I hung out with him, me being so old and him being so young, but he was like a young me, except when I was his age I was more badass. We wanted to get high. However, he, like always, was broke, and I, on the other hand, had only enough for one forty-ounce. I couldn't drink, though. I would get violently ill. I'd been prescribed antabuse, a drug designed to counter nature, to stop alcoholics from drinking. People **can** die from drinking on antabuse, but that was rare, although I didn't want to find out exactly how rare that was. I had been told it feels like you're dying, only you don't die. So I would avoid alcohol altogether. I wouldn't even put it on my skin, or else I would develop a painful rash. One night when I'd stayed in a hotel with my dad, he had commented on the stench rising from my boots. What can I say? He had bought me this spray, which contained a high level of ether, to rid my boots of that awful stench. After wearing my boots for four days my feet had begun to itch and burn. Upon removing my boots I had uncovered a terrible rash: both my feet were bright red with white spots all over and had looked like Ruffles potato chips. I had seen what antabuse can do.

With only four dollars—**my** money—between the two of us, DXM was our only option. So we went to the Walgreens across the street from where I had used to live. If I had still lived in that shithole, I would have suggested we rip off Walmart. But Walgreens was easy; the only girl working was sixteen-years old, small, fragile. I wore my tight straight-leg blue jeans, cuffed at the bottom, flashing my tall heavy steel-toed red-straight-laced Doctor Martins, my black hoody zipped up, the hood over my head, and to conceal my identity pitch-black sunglasses wrapped around my face. I looked scary. No one in Rutland, Vermont—or anywhere, for that matter—would have dared to fuck with me, especially not a young girl straight out of high school. Not going to happen.

What happened next was badass, although Brendan was a pussy. I wanted him to steal the Triple C's because if he got caught, the law would go easier on him ["Go in there—I'll create a distraction—and steal two boxes," I said, "one for me and one for you. That's sixteen pills each" / "Why me?" he replied, uncooperative / "Because you're only sixteen, that's why. The law would go easier on you" / "I'm not doing it. No way, man" / "Fuck it! I'll do it"].

I pulled it off. I stole two boxes, without any help from Brendan—piece of cake, no planning necessary—in only four simple steps: (1) Walk into the store followed by Brendan and march directly to the medicine aisle, losing Brendan to the store. (2) Locate the cough medicine section. (3) Bend down, displace two boxes of Triple C's from the shelf—the second shelf from the bottom—then stand up.

(4) Holding the boxes in your right hand a few inches from your right hip, leave the store, walking right past the check-out counter on your right, the girl watching as you go, the camera recording as you open the door casually, your pace speeding up rapidly as the door shuts behind you. Then I bolted, coming to a halt as I crossed over the border of the Walgreens parking lot, Brendan waiting for my arrival (the last I had remembered, he had been in the store). A successful robbery, it was indeed.

On the way back to my apartment, creeping through the backstreets, we spotted three police cruisers on the prowl. For each cruiser we ducked into bushes or hid behind trees, making sure we were not spotted incase those cruisers were for us. A wave of paranoia—why we had taken the deserted backstreets, the long way home—sifted through our insides. I was easily recognizable, especially for a small city like Rutland, but hard to spot in the dark. Brendan, however, had worn brighter colors, and although he hadn't stolen the pills he had walked into the store with me and had most likely been recorded on camera.

We tripped crazily that night; he'd taken half a box—eight pills—and I'd taken one and a half—twenty-four pills—stirring my imagination like crazy [I said: "What doesn't kill you is a great big disappointment." Then: "If you attempt suicide and live through it, that sucks. Like, if you fail, that's terrible"]. I took a sip of my water [then, after a brief pause, said: "Like, you try to kill yourself by getting hit by a car, right? What if you don't die? What if you live? / "Then," Brendan chimed in, swaying his head left and right, bug-eyed, "you just get hit by a car"]. I turned my head to look right, investigating Brendan ["Yea, then you suffer. Yea, you get casted, and all that shit; you suffer … and … and, uh …" I added, incoherently thinking about what to say next. "You take a bottle of pills, you just get your stomach pumped. You cut your wrists, you just get … bandages"]. Brendan was rubbing his head throughout my speech, still rubbing it [when he said: "Jump off a train," and half mumbled, "and you'll kill yourself" / "Yea …" I mumbled back, looking away from him, "that may work…. I was talking to this girl earlier today…. She said: 'Why'd you wanna kill yourself. You love yourself'"]. Brendan continued rubbing his head, only half tuned in to what I was saying but not comprehending a single word ["It's not that …" I continued. "It's not that I … it's not that I wanna kill myself, 'cause I love myself. I love myself. But I **hate** everybody … around me"]. Fiddling with my water bottle, I looked at my feet. Brendan cocked his head, resting his head on his shoulder, watching as I talked ["I can't stand being in this world," I continued. "This world is like … so like … alien to me" / "Aliens," he shrieked, startled / "Do you know what I mean," I raised my voice, "this world is so fucking alien to me? And it sucks," I wined, placing my water on the coffee table].

I gave myself a haircut that night, butchering my hair, looking like I had gotten my ass kicked by a badger. I took my clippers, in a fit of rage, and proceeded to stab my head in many places, cutting my hair all over. The following Monday when Allan had first laid eyes on me he flipped out ["**What the fuck were you thinking?!**" he yelled. "**How the fuck are you going to get a fuckin' job now?! You fuckin'—**" / "I was high," I mumbled under my breath, too quiet for him to hear / "**—idiot!**" he continued. "**What the fuck?!**

Fuck, fuck, fuck," he went on, "**blah, blah, blah!**" / "I was high," I confessed, this time loud enough for him to hear, foiling his rant].

As Brendan slowly waved his hand in front of his face, I crept over to my computer, peering at the screen through Chinese eyes ["I'm gonna play a good song," I said, tuned in to my computer, searching for a good song / "Dude, I'm trippin' nuts," Brendan told me, eyes wide and bulging / "I'm gonna play a good song," I reiterated / and then he reminded me: "Dude, I'm trippin' nuts" / "I'm gonna play a good song" / "All right, good," he said, totally spaced, cocking his head back, smoking a cigarette, blowing smoke rings. "Dude … Jay …" / "What?" / "I'm trippin' fuckin' nuts" / "Yea, but you didn't take as much as me" / "I know, but I'm still trippin' sack-hole, dude"].

The following Monday after Alan had seen my new haircut he had a fit. I explained to him that I was high ["Why?" he asked / "I'm an addict" / "That's no excuse. Do you think, thirty years from now, you can just say, 'I'm an addict,' and people will excuse you? No! Of course they won't" / "I'm not making any excuses. That's just what happened" / "Get a fucking haircut!" he commanded]. A haircut. Great! Can you believe not a single Barber Shop opens on Mondays? ["It's an old tradition," a woman told me]. Fuck traditions! So I brought my clippers to Sam's apartment, where he shaved my head.

A few days later I nearly got into a fight with a middle-aged overweight asshole. He was pissed because, apparently, his wife had given him shit about God knows what. I walked by his house minding my own business, my boom box dangling from my right hand ["**Shut that shit off!**" I heard somebody yell]. I turned to look left [and said: "Fuck off!"] as a small man strutted across the walkway leading to the street. He yelled at me, complaining about the noise, and I yelled back, telling him to mind his own fucking business and fuck off. This went on for five to ten minutes ["This is stupid," I declared], and then I spit in his face, walked away ["If you do that again," came from behind me, "I'll kick your ass"]. I had it with that fucktard. I turned around and marched straight at him, stopping before I would have knocked him over, looking down as he looked up at me, scared ["I just did"]. Then I turned back around, leaving the little man behind.

Next something weird happened as I walked away ["Who are you listening to?" came from behind me]. Turning around [I said: "What?"], I stopped, eyeballing the strange man, unsure of what to think ["Who are you listening to?" / "MDC. Why?"]. As the man walked toward me ["They're good"] I stood still, bewildered ["Right," I mumbled]. Then I turned around, the man to my right, a little behind me, hiding in my shadow as we walked, buddy-buddy all of a sudden ["Sorry about earlier," he said. "It's just, you know, the wife" / "Yep," I replied, not really caring / "I'm mike"]. He offered me his hand, and I looked at him [wanting to say, *Are you fucking kidding me?* but I kept quite because my eyes said it all / "You seem like the kind of guy who doesn't back down easily" / "Yep" / "I was intimidated. That's for sure" / "Yep" / "The way you got in my face like that. I was scared" / "Yep"]. We approached an intersection, and I turned left ["I'm going this way," he said, pointing straight, as I walked away. "Bye"]. He waved,

I think, but I'm not entirely sure, as I wondered what the fuck had just happened back there. What a freak!

A week later I got hit by a car while riding my bike. I got tossed three feet through the air and landed on my back.

Earlier I received a phone call from Mikey [**ring, ring!** / "Hello?" I said / "Hey, man, it's Mikey" / "I have caller ID. What's up?" / "I have two hexagons I need to get rid of" / "How much?" / "Ten bucks"]. That got my attention ["Ten bucks?" / "Meet me in front of Walgreens in fifteen minutes" / "Fifteen minutes?" / "Fifteen minutes, Jay. No later" / "That's a twenty-five-minute walk. At least" / "I don't care. Ride your bike" / "Have you been outside today?" I queried. "It's freezing" / "You're on the clock! Fifteen minutes" / "But—"]. He hung up. Fuck, I gotta go! I hurriedly threw on my black hoody, then my flannel, then my leather bomber jacket, then my scaly cap, flipping my hood over my head, slid my wallet into my back pocket, slipped on my shoes, as if they were sandals, pocketed my keys, opened and closed my door before one could say "büpe," and I hopped on my bike, rode to the end of my drive way, freezing my nuts off, my gloveless hands numb, taking a right turn, switching to my lowest gear, and pedaled downhill, quickly approaching a deserted intersection (this all happened at night). As I crossed the deserted intersection—[**smash!**]—

I quickly got up (my many layers—especially my leather jacket—had worked as body armor) and was back on my bike, pedaling away [when I heard: "Are you all right?"]. Not wanting to raise any more suspicion, I stopped my bike. To my right a Good-Samaritan had pulled over to check if I was all right, if I was hurt ["Yea, I'm fine. No big deal"]. I started pedaling again, keeping a steady pace, not to act too suspicious [but then the good-Samaritan said: "He pulled over"]. He pointed behind me, where the asshole that had hit me had pulled over, waiting to see if I was okay, waiting to protect his ass. I was not interested in suing anybody. I just wanted my drugs, and they were taking up my valuable time, although I didn't want the cops called. No way. So I backtracked [wanting to say, *Leave me the fuck alone. You hit me. That's bad enough. Now you wanna waste my valuable fucking time. Fuck off!* / "I didn't see you there," the man said]. He **had** tried to stop. He had slammed on the breaks, otherwise I would be creamed. He just was not fast enough, I guessed. I would cut him a break, I decided [and said: "Don't worry about it! You did try to—" / "Are you hurt?" the asshole interrupted, pretending to care / "I'm fine," I said, as I mounted my bike. "Not a big deal"].

I rode away, arriving at Walgreens a couple minutes late as Mikey was walking away, heading home, I assumed. I rode my bike up to him, cutting him off ["Just barely made it, Jay," he said. "You're lucky"]. Then I bought the büpe.

I placed one suboxone beneath my tongue and headed home. On my way home [**ring, ring!**] Sam called me ["What's up?" he said / "Just heading home" / "You think you could buy me beer?"]. Sam was only nineteen ["No, not tonight" / "Okay" / a brief pause, then: "I'll do you one better," I said in a giving spirit / "What's that?" / "I'll give you half a suboxone"]. That night was the best in Sam's life, I can guarantee. Too bad it would **never** happen again, at least not with my contribution.

And, oh yea, I can't forget about this: One morning while walking to get my meds, a van pulled up to me ["Freak!" the passenger yelled]. As the van pulled away I tossed my lit cigarette through the driver's side window. Seriously! The cigarette butt flew right through the window. I was surprised myself, but proud. I bragged about that to everybody all day long.

I FELT TIRED, WORN OUT from all the drugs and lack of sleep I had gotten in the past few days. *Family Guy* ended, and I thought: *I wouldn't mind passing out to a movie tonight*. I reached under my couch, where I found a black CD book, which looked like a briefcase, filled with half of my DVD collection—the other half was in another similar CD book. Then I propped the CD book on my lap, skimmed through my DVDs, indecisively searching for a movie to watch. I picked out *Rock and Rolla*. I walked to my TV, opened my DVD player, inserted the disc, and then sat back down as I pressed PLAY on the remote control. Fifteen minutes into the movie I lit a cigarette.

I finished the cigarette in five minutes, and then ... then everything faded to black.

Chapter 5: My New Resolve

WE ARE RIDING THE TRAIN *through Boston and riding the green line and Rebecca and Timmy and I are riding the train and passing around a two-liter bottle of coke and whiskey and riding the train and laughing and talking and drinking through Boston and Rebecca and Timmy and I are preparing for the night ahead and riding the train and into Cambridge we arrive at Harvard Square* *drunk as skunks and I'm seated on a concrete bench in the pit wasted and then a group of four or five or six (I'm too drunk to count) Punks appear from around the corner and nod,* Up the Punks, *at us so we—Rebecca and Timmy and I—nod back in unisons and a bond has been established and then a gorgeous girl separates herself from the pack of Punks coming our way ["Jay!" she screams gleefully] lunging forward and landing on my lap [wondering why Colin's girlfriend is all over me, "Are you still going out with Colin?" I ask her / "What? I'm not going out with Colin"] so then I grab the back of her head smashing our faces together and our lips meet and our tongues touch and we become one ["What the fuck?!" I hear someone say] for only a few seconds and then I detach myself from her and look up and it's David and he is looking down at me grinning ["What the fuck is your problem, man?!" he says with deadly force / "What are you talking about?" I ask, slightly confused / "This is your third fuckin' strike" / "What?" Still confused] and then Rebecca grabs David before he would have struck me ["Oooohh," I moan, like I suddenly understand, then add, "I thought she was Colin's girlfriend. That's why I asked her, 'Are you going out with Colin?' and she said, 'I'm not going out with Colin,' so I thought.... I didn't know—" / "Fuck you, man!" he snaps / "Chill out, dude," Rebecca says, holding David back. "It was a mistake. You know Jay. He can be an idiot at times" / "This is his third strike" / "What do you mean, 'third strike'?" I ask / "The third fuckin' time you hit on Lily, and this time you kissed her" / "What the fuck? I never even met her before. I thought she was Colin's girlfriend" / "You hit on her—"] and then Mike grabs David by his shoulder [and says: "Let's go"] and pulls him away ["—on your fucking birthday," David continues. "Last Halloween"],* David wants to fight me, let him, I'll kick his fucking teeth in, *and then we all walk along Mass Ave. heading toward Central Square to the show David leading the pack and Timmy and I follow from the rear and with David still screaming about me kissing Colin's girlfriend I look up at the sky [and scream: "**We are the hardest band in Boston. The Moral Defects. MD 77,**" proud of myself. "**We live faster; we play louder**"] feeling godly and Timmy and I slap hands,* We rule OK, *but the night is still young and then we walk past a sex shop which catches my attention and my head turns to look at the store but my feet continue walking and then come to a stop and I take two steps backwards so I'm parallel with the sex shop looking inside and although the store is closed the gate is open just enough so I can duck right under and Timmy does just that: he ducks under the gate and opens the door slightly ["Jay, it's open," he informs me] and I take his lead and now I am under the gate and through the front door and Timmy stays outside watching for police or anyone else who might bring trouble our way and the store is stacked with porn DVDs all around the walls and racks of porn magazines and sex toys everywhere else and a half-open door at the far end possibly leading to the basement catches my attention so my body tightens,* I'm not alone, *and I can hear trickles of laughter coming through the door and the smell of weed is coming through the door,* The store clerks are down there, smoking weed, *and my nerves race through my veins sending out warnings and telling me to* **Get out!** *and they might not have closed the gate all the way because* **They're still in the store**, *and then I come to* *the sharp realization that* **I'm not supposed to be in here**, I'm out of my league, *and I stand still frozen solid my head shifting left and right and scanning the store like an owl searching for prey,* I could get arrested for a nighttime B&E, what was I thinking? but it's too late to turn around, I'm already in here, *and in my drunken haze I grab the first thing I can get a hold of—a bondage belt—and then make a quick exit afraid I might get caught out the door and under the gate where Timmy waits for my departure and I shake off my anxiety and we bolt catching up to the pack and as we catch up to everyone else ["Jay, can I see?" Rebecca asks me] I pass the belt to Rebecca never laying eyes on it again although a block up Rebecca passes me a five-dollar bill ["David bought the belt for five dollars"] and I slip the bill into my pocket unaware of its origins ["Thanks"] and then we all drink more and I stand outside the show swaying with the wind and Timmy and Timmy and two girls I don't recognize ...* two girls? ... *focus! ... Timmy and a girl I don't recognize his arm wrapped around her holding her dearly and both grinning drunkenly like two newfound lovers come over to me ["Jay, this is ... this is ... Michelle," Timmy sort of spits] and I offer my hand ["Nice to* ***hiccup!*** *meet—"] and fall forward and then—[**crash!**]—*

I walk along Mass Ave. with Rebecca and Antichristina, What just happened? *and then ["I definitely like you better," Antichristina tells me, "when we're not at my place"] we turn right onto a back street and Rebecca [who says: "It's open"] opens a car door and I steal the stereo and I'm outside the show where a big crowd of Punks surrounds the door ["You wanna buy a car stereo?" I ask someone. "You wanna buy a car stereo?" I ask someone else] and people* *give me a what-the-fuck-is-wrong-with-you? kind of look so I toss the stereo into a nearby dumpster and then [**ring, ring!**] my phone rings [**ring, ring!**] and I answer it ["Hello?" / "I'm gonna rape your girlfriend" / "Who the fuck is this?!" / "The police"],* The police, fucking pigs, I'll kill all of you, *and then outside the show the crowd still lingering and a cop standing by ["**You fucking bastard!**" I yell at the cop. "**What do you mean you're gonna rape my girlfriend?! You fucking cunt! I'll fucking kill you!**"] Eric grabs me by my shoulder [and asks: "What the hell are you doing?"] and pulls me into the crowd and—*

*I zigzag along Mass Ave. minding my o—[**whack!**]—*

*A fist crashes into my face knocking me on my back and I lay on the side of the street and a foot stomps on my stomach and then kicks me in the head and then a fist crashes into my jaw as I lay there getting beaten not a clue to what's going on and numb to the pain and then a second person joins in on my agony and two feet descend upon me with jolting force and fists come flying down and kick-punch-stomp-kick-kick-stomp-punch-[**crack!**]-punch-stomp-stomp-punch-kick and then my attackers bolt and I can hear their feet sounding like a drum roll and beating the ground as they run,* Where was Rebecca when all that happened?

MY EYES OPENED. THEN I sat up immediately, sweat beating down my face. *Fuck, it was only a dream. Thank God! Oh no!* My stomach churned. I stood up and flew into the bathroom, landing on my knees, my head hovering over the toilet bowl. My stomach exploded outward, discharge spraying into the toilet like an upside-down geyser.

The spray stopped, and … I was at it again, dry-heaving—nothing left inside. I was on my knees for ten, maybe fifteen or twenty minutes. Then I stood up, glanced into the mirror, where I saw my reflection—not a pretty sight: my pale face, my red eyes, and a string of saliva dripped from my mouth, stretching out, growing longer. Then I wiped my mouth clean on my sleeve.

I slowly walked, in a stupor, out of my bathroom feeling terrible. *I wish Rebecca was here.* I sat in front of my computer half-asleep, logged onto my email account, and … *no way!* My eyes widened: she had responded. A surge of utter happiness jolted me awake. Anticipation and excitement and nervous anxiety…. *She had written back. Finally!*

Hey, it's great to hear from you.

It's great to hear from you too!

Hey, it's great to hear from you.

I'm psyched to hear you're doing well. I would be nothing but glad to talk to you. The only problem is, I have classes, and finals are coming up. I'm afraid you might distract me, which I can't afford right now. I have a 4.0 GPA, and I hope to keep that up. Sorry! Finals, however, will be over in, say, a month. Maybe we can talk then. Maybe! A very big maybe! Keep doing what you've been doing, and we'll talk later.

Love, Rebecca.

One month! It was then and there when my life took an unexpected turn. No one could have predicted what came next. That email changed my life. *I refuse to be strung out when I talk to Rebecca*, I decided. *I simply refuse. No way*. I would have died, I'm guessing, two to three years later if it had not been for that email. Sobriety, I declared. Recovery, I set out for. First thing Monday morning I would confess to Alan that I had been using suboxone under the radar for all those months, and stealing Ritalin and Klonopin to ingest nasally. I needed help, I realized for the first time ever. No, I knew I needed help. I hadn't been willing to accept help. *Fuck your help!* is what I had thought. But no more. From then on I would ask for help, I would listen to the suggestions, and to the best of my ability I would follow the suggestions. My way had always screwed me over. I would go to Twelve Step meetings and I would work the Twelve Steps with a sponsors. But that would all come later. Now I would tell Alan the truth. First thing Monday morning. Tonight, however, I would get high. One last time!

A Tribute to Lethal Erection

[We lived faster, we played louder....]

TO JEREMY ACID (GUITAR), HARRY Erection (bass guitar), Johnny Pain (drums), Fat Pat (drums), Sick Boy (drums), Pissed Off Jay (bass guitar), Mike (drums), and Cardinal Erection (drums); but mostly to De-Chuck-Tive (guitar) and Kristen Epileptic (bass guitar).

The Complete Songs

Anti-Social

Baby, Don't Tease

Deranged

Don't Go to Boston

Drunken Fun

Eat Shit

Fight for Equality

Gotta Finda Way

Homeless

I Love You

I Masturbate

Lethal Erection

Lose Control

Pretty Faces

JEREMY VOID

The Show Tonight
Wake and Shake

FIND EVERY SONG ON YOUTUBE now.

About the Author

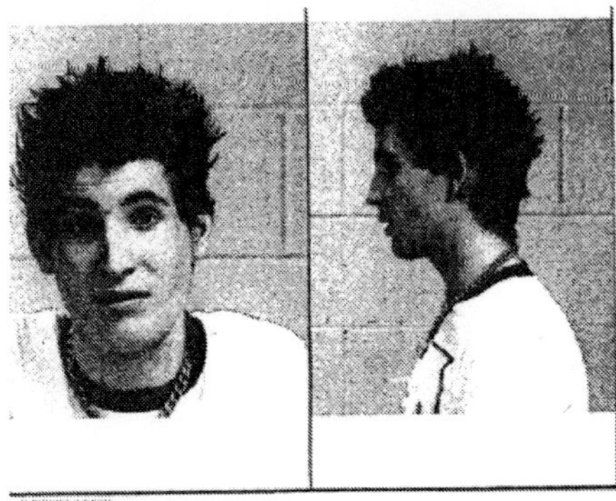

JEREMY VOID WAS BORN AND raised in Boston, MA, where he played in a Punk rock band called Lethal Erection and stirred up chaos everywhere he went. Friends, enemies, and followers alike called him "St. Chaos," and he kept up his reputation at all times, finding the funny side of just about everything, and leading a life of misadventures that eventually led him down a rocky road to Rutland, VT, where he resides for the time being, writing short stories.

Be sure to visit

www.chaoswriting.com

to find out about any news pertaining to *Derelict America* or Jeremy Void himself.